# Diamonds Are for Trevor

A comic adventure story

By

Barry Childs

Disclaimer

Any similarity to actual places, events, or characters (living or dead) in this novel is absolutely deliberate. Any similarity with fictitious places, events, or characters (living or dead!) is purely coincidental.

2nd edition. Revised 2018
Published by Reference Point, France
Printed in Poland by Amazon Fulfillment


Acknowledgements:
**Bernard (Byn) Walters** for proof-reading, technical help, and historical corrections.
**Frances Brightman**, my second in command, for reading early drafts and for helping with the cover. Oh, and for all that tea.
**Professor David Jenkins** and **Anita Heward** for their encouragement and advice.

***Fantasy drives the hypocrite and fool***
***Into thinking he's one step ahead***
***But when the dawn breaks, and he finally awakes***
***He will find himself still in his bed***

Trefor Dylan Jones

**WARNING**

This novel contains strong language unsuitable for children, childish humour unsuitable for adults, scenes of violence unsuitable for lily-livered wimps, and no sex.

This book may also cause offence if you are;

Algerian, American, Australian, Bahamian, Belgian, Breton, Chinese, Congolese, Dutch, English, French, German, Irish, Italian, Scottish, Spanish, Vaticanian, or indeed even Welsh.
(Listed in alphabetical order to aid the Irish).

You may also be upset if you are;

Hindu, Jewish, Methodist, Muslim, Roman Catholic, Gay, Straight, or bi-sexual.

I assume there are a few hardened criminals from The Democratic Republic of Congo who will still want to continue reading. Believe me, it's not worth it. You would get more pleasure watching a snail run a marathon.

(Please add Congolese to the list of nationalities above)

# Prologue

Bryn had never jumped a red light before, but this was an exceptional day. They arrived at the hospital just in time. Two men ran to the car with a trolley bed and hoisted Glynis onto it. They rushed her into ward four. She was screaming and crying. Her face screwed up with pain. The midwife suggested breathing exercises and started breathing heavily along with Glynis. Bryn was confused, who in hell was having the baby? There was suddenly a great gush of water. Bryn shrieked. The midwife and nurse were telling her to push. 'C'mon Glynis, I need you to push. Push. Push.'

Half an hour passed, and everyone was sweating and shouting push. A little head finally looked out as if to say, *What's all the fuss about*? A camel had gone through the eye of a needle.

Glynis Jones gave birth to Trefor Dylan Jones in Prince Charles Hospital, Merthyr Tydfil, on Wednesday the first of April 1987. Her husband, Bryn, said it was a miracle. It would not be long before he regretted using those words.

***

Daffydd Llewellyn had been Trevor's best friend since Primary school, and both lived in the same street, Azalea Park in Upper Dowlais, a district of Merthyr Tydfil.

The two boys went to the same two schools, Cyfarthfa Park Primary, and Heolgerrig Community. Neither of them made it to the County Grammar School due to sickness, diagnosed by Trevor's mother as being an acute form of the mental disease lazyitis.

In his early teens, Trevor had developed a flair for writing poetry and assumed that one day he would be a famous poet. His parents, who taught English, thought not. By the grace of God for Trevor, they taught in Cardiff.

When his father wasn't working, he was playing golf at Pant Golf Club. When his mother wasn't working, she was clearing up after Trevor.

David's parents had a successful printing business, Copy and Paste, and occasionally they would ask him to help in the printing room, but David was always busy with his homework. Apparently, his maths teacher suggested the Racing Post as the perfect research tool for analysis and calculation. Lazyitis was indeed a severe disease.

The two boys spent their secondary-school days dreaming up ideas for becoming rich, none of which worked or indeed involved work.

A somewhat, introverted young man, David enjoyed doing little else apart from watching horse racing and rugby. Due to his illness, he never played rugby, so his chances of becoming famous like his namesake, Tommy David, were zero.

***

Dowlais, a village in the county borough of Merthyr Tydfil, had a close-knit community which revolved around the choir, Cor Meibion Dowlais. That is to us English speakers, Dowlais Male Voice Choir. The choir was the hub, and if you didn't sing in it, then someone in your family did.

Dowlais has a rich history and is famous for once having the largest ironworks in the world, the Dowlais Iron Company, which employed over 5,000 people. Many celebrities came from or lived in Dowlais. The singer Robert Rees and the actor Richard Harrington. The famous lawyer David William Evans, known for his rugby skills. The actor Richard Davies, and most famous of all, the fashion designer Laura Ashley.

***

Trevor took a keen interest in conjuring, or to be more precise, vanishing things. His grandfather, who lived nearby in Pen-y-Darren, had been an amateur magician and hypnotist for many years. He taught his grandson sleight of hand and was relieved to see this intricate craft passed on to another generation of his family, who would use it to entertain and amaze the masses. Little did he know!

Hypnotism had no appeal for Trevor. He just didn't believe in it. His grandfather insisted that he had hypnotised Trevor many times, but his grandson would be unaware of this. Trevor thought it was all nonsense and preferred the excitement of vanishing things. After school, he would go with David to the corner shop on Heolgerrig Road and vanish a few chocolate bars. David always waited outside the shop. It made him nervous. On one occasion the vanish of a Mars Bar was unsuccessful. The bar fell onto the floor just as

Mister Jenkins was peering over the counter at him. Mister Jenkins knew the family and accepted Trevor's apology and explanation that he had been under hypnosis at the time.

One thing Trevor did excel in, was his ability to recall by association. Another trick his grandfather had taught him. He would use this method to enable him to remember the order of half a pack of playing cards, and the words to several songs. After hearing a song just a few times Trevor was able to remember it, but often forgot to go to school! He invented (or stole) quotes and pithy one-liners, and memorised them, and used them when he thought proper or inappropriate, depending on his mood.

Trevor entertained his friend by performing card tricks. The Three-card Monty was his speciality. He also taught himself and David to play Gin Rummy. Due to Trevor's excellent memory, they were hard to beat. They would hitch a ride to Pontypridd or Abergavenny to play as the residents of Merthyr had already succumbed to their exploits. Opponents soon ran out in these small towns too, and they had to travel to Cardiff to find new opposition. Playing Rummy was one of the rare occasions when they *earned* their money.

David loved to sing, but unlike Trevor, it took him ages to learn a song. One song he had memorised, *Take Me Home*, he sang all day to everyone's annoyance.

Apart from their moneymaking projects, David's interests were rugby, music, and horse-racing, in that order. He wanted to travel, but because his parents were in business, the family never went far on holidays. Each year they would go to Snowdonia and walk up and down hills singing The Grand Old Duke of York. As far as David was concerned, this was as boring as it gets. David's parents excused him from taking holidays with them when he reached his sixteenth birthday.

Another of his Father's ideas that made his parents more enthusiastic about going.

David loved rugby, and he often walked into Merthyr to watch The Ironmen play. That was the local name for Merthyr RFC. Pen-y-Darren stood halfway between Dowlais and Merthyr, so he and Trevor walked together to Pen-y-Darren where Trevor then went to visit his grandad, while David carried on to Merthyr to watch the rugby. They would later meet in Pen-y-Darren to get up to no good.

One of Trevor's favourite pastimes was to nick milk from the milk-van, and then sell it to the kids in Pen-y-Darren school. It was his dad's idea, or so he liked to think. His dad told him that not long before Trevor was born the milkman used to use a horse-drawn milk cart and it was commonplace to follow it with a shovel and scoop up the horse's dung to fertilise the vegetable plot. Trevor was sure that between his father and grandfather they had coerced him into being dishonest. He never intended becoming a crook, he believed it was in his genes. His mother always said, *Trevor, if you want to stay out of trouble, keep it in your genes.*

***

# Chapter 1

## There Are No Brains in London

Trevor stumbled across his first means of proper employment at the tender age of seventeen. His grandfather taught him the technique for removing someone's wristwatch or pocket watch. The targeted person would never know their beloved timepiece had gone. It was all a matter of distraction, and the ability to carry out the single-handed clasp twists.

There are four of these, depending on the type of band or bracelet the victim was wearing. It took many months before Trevor became adept at all four. Once he had achieved this, it was only a matter of time before his new-found hobby became a living. David helped with the distraction but felt uncomfortable with this and believed Trevor was heartless. Trevor found that amusing.

On Saturdays, they travelled to Cardiff by train to vanish a few watches. The next day they would go to the pubs in Newport to sell them and drink their favourite beer, Brains bitter. On the odd occasion, they would find a couple of stooges and make a few shillings playing Rummy.

David loved the word *combine*. He would use it a lot. When they went to the pub, David always wanted to combine their cash. Trevor usually lost out as he generally had more money than David. It worried Trevor whenever David said the word combine.
They were always short of cash. The trouble with South Wales is that most people are on a low-income and are reluctant to part with their hard-earned money. After train fares, beer, and David's gambling on dogs and horses, profit was minimal or non-existent.

Trevor often entertained with card tricks and made a few pounds performing his Three-card Monty on Merthyr High Street during the week in the summer. He then squandered his ill-gotten gains in the Tredegar Arms.
David's father tried to coerce his son into joining his printing company but to no avail. Trevor agreed with David's father. It was a terrific opportunity. The idea of falsifying passports and other essential documents appealed to him. It would be easier than working down Ffos-y-fran mine, or St. Merryn Meats, or selling ice-cream in Giovanni's Parlour!

***

David enjoyed listening to the local choir. It must have been the combined voices. The choir practised on Thursdays from 7 pm, in the Dowlais Centenary Hall, and welcomed anyone who wanted to listen or to sing along. He would often go and sing along to *Take Me Home*, his favourite song. It was also an opportunity to meet friends and relatives who sang in the choir.

His father was a vice-president. It sounded very grand and demanded respect from the choristers, but all it really meant was that he gave them an annual donation, and in return, the choir would advertise Copy and Paste in their concert programmes.

The choir travelled to many countries including America, Canada, Holland, France, and Italy. They have won the National Eisteddfod and represented Wales twice at the International Celtic Festival in Lorient, France. The choir have sung at famous places such as the Champs Elyse in Paris, The Millennium Stadium, St Paul's Cathedral, and The Royal Albert Hall in London. They have been on television programmes and sung with distinguished soloists like Katherine Jenkins, Haley Westenra, Bryn Terfel, and Donny Osmond. In 1998, astronaut Daffydd Rhys Williams took a recording of the choir into space on the Columbia Shuttle. Dylan Thomas wrote about the tenors of Dowlais in his *play for voices*, Under Milk Wood. Trevor thought that was impressive.

As the choir was desperate for new, younger members, they invited David to join. At eighteen he was the youngest member of Cor Meibion Dowlais. He couldn't sing, but if he visited Cardiff Park not knowing the words to Hen Wlad Fy Nhadau (Land of My Fathers), it might get ugly. Trevor had no such problem at rugby matches due to his ability to remember the words to almost any song.

David had another reason to sing, travel. If you attended choir regularly and were not tone-deaf, it cost nothing to travel with them on their tours. As the choir was a registered charity, donations paid for all travel expenses. Trevor always said *charity begins at home*, so David knew he must make the most of this. He attended choir as often as he could, as only the diehards were offered the opportunity to travel. The choir achieved first prize at the National Eisteddfod in Ruthin, but

David’s name had not been on the list of selected singers. He reasoned this must be due to the tailors, as he hadn’t received his uniform yet. The Musical Director told him that was not the problem, it was because they didn't want to be laughed off the stage. David wasn't sure if that had been a joke!

***

Finally, in March, he did take part in a joint concert with the famous London Welsh Choir. The choir went to North London and stayed in a luxurious hotel for two nights. It wasn't his angelic, dulcet tones that got him to London. It was because the Musical Director, Cyril Davies, held the post of senior manager at Copy and Paste. David's father gave Cyril a choice. ‘David goes to London or your demoted.’ David went to London.

He looked smart in his new uniform. White shirt, black tie, and black trousers and jacket. The jacket was embroidered with the distinguished logo that looked like a dragon perched on top of a chimney.

The coach journey was fun. They all had a sing-song and a few drinks to pass the time away. When they reached the hotel, David went straight to bed with a headache. The joint concert the next day went very well although Cyril Davies was not happy with the London Welsh’s gaudy red jackets. David was miming most of the time. After the concert, he and Dai Ferguson, a seventy-year-old half Scot from Aberdare, spent half the night in the hotel, singing *Take Me Home* with three members of The London Welsh Choir.

Brains beer was unheard of in North London, so David had to make do drinking whisky with Dai, after combining their cash.

David suffered from travel sickness, whisky sickness and lazyitis, so the combination proved to be a disaster. The driver stopped the coach several times during the return journey!

When David got home and informed Trevor that he could not find any Brains beer in London, Trevor simplified it and claimed it as his latest one-liner. *There are no Brains in London.*

***

# 1966

## (Remind me again?)

In merry England memories are rife
Of Wembley's green and pleasant lawn
When Germans were crushed to remind the world
Of England's might and brawn

But here in the mountains grey and damp
We grieve and sing for our young lost souls
Rock and shale, slurry, and mud
We recall our kids as England recalls its goals

No, this is not a bitter cry
For I too am an England fan
But only one hundred-and-sixty miles
Separate Wembley from Aberfan

Trefor Dylan Jones 2018

# Chapter 2

Timepiece Crime

While David sang his little heart out in London, Trevor was at home planning their biggest job so far. When they were selling watches in Newport, they found that many punters wanted up-market brands such as Rolex or Omega, and these watches demanded good money. Several makes of watches were worth Thousands of pounds if you can find a buyer. They had a client list. The most sought-after wristwatch was the ultra-flash Rolex Day-Date, and Trevor had been watching one for a while.

Trevor knew a car dealer and entrepreneur in Newport, Maldwyn Davies. He had met him in The Man of Gwent pub while playing Rummy there. Maldwyn had cottoned on to Trevor's ability to remember the order of playing cards and intended to profit by it. Maldwyn owned the Grosvenor casino and offered Trevor a well-paid position as croupier or card sharp as Trevor preferred to call himself. He would have jumped at the chance had it not been for an old friend, John Roberts, who overheard the conversation and took him to one side and discouraged him after telling him in some detail what a ruthless man Mr Davies was. John had worked for Maldwyn Davies in the chip exchange office and since leaving had developed a twinge in his right eye. He blamed it on stress. John knew of at least two croupier's who disappeared after openly saying that they were reporting him for unethical business activities.

Trevor kept on the right side of Maldwyn who was on his client list, and who was willing to pay a fair price for a Rolex Day-Date. Maldwyn looked and acted like a real gangster. He was a big ugly man who wore a mohair suit with a white tie and ridiculous looking white shoes.

Trevor went to see him at the car lot and told him he had the opportunity to get a Day-Date. As a gesture of goodwill, he gave Trevor a five-hundred-pound deposit, which Trevor safely stowed under his pillow until such time that they had completed the deal.

When David returned from choir duty, Trevor explained the plan to him. David was not impressed. 'That was stupid Trev, I've only been away for a few days, and I come home to find I've joined a ring of organised crime. Accepting a deposit from a gangster is like signing your own death certificate, Oh, and incidentally, mine too.'

Trevor shrugged. 'I know he's not a pheasant plucker, but he's a car dealer, not the bloody godfather.'

'Oh yea, Well Trev, I noticed you were in no hurry to take his two-hundred quid a week to work in his casino, Did you?'

'Were you, David. The correct grammar is, were you.'

'Were you, and where were you when he invited us to the party at his mansion?'

‘I was busy doing nothing. Don’t worry my little raspberry fruitcake. I’ll sort the deal out with the gangster. You just concentrate on the job at hand. We leave for sunny Cardiff in the morning, and then we shall be as rich as milk Sheiks, or even oil Sheiks’

***

The two superheroes swung into action. Cardiff's Duke Street Arcade was home to Goldsmith's Jewellers, where the two Welsh thieves intended a daylight robbery. The plan was for David to use his distracting skills while Trevor vanished away a Rolex Oyster Day-Date.

They had already calculated that the best time for the job was on a Saturday morning when the crowded streets would ease the getaway. The watches were in the front window, near the door, and there was no back to the display. It would be a simple matter of David keeping the assistant busy finding the perfect engagement ring that his soon to be wife wanted to buy him. Trevor would, at the crucial time snatch the wristwatch and run. Nothing could be easier! They would meet up with Maldwyn at The Tredegar Arms in the evening to conclude the transaction.

They took the X4 bus to Cardiff on a lovely sunny Saturday morning. David was always nervous, but Trevor never suffered from nerves. Trevor said, ‘We will have to watch our timing.’ That was one of his little jokes.

They both wore sunglasses for a partial disguise. Opposite the jewellers was Starbucks coffee shop. An ideal place to wait for the best opportunity to act. They sat in the window seat wearing dark glasses and suits. They looked more like *The Blues Brothers* than professional jewel thieves.

David would not buy coffee here because he had read that Starbucks had been cheating the treasury out of tax! They waited until there were no customers in the shop. Trevor said, 'It's time to strike, we don't have a minute to spare. I'll keep watch.'

David was not impressed, 'Was that another one of your stupid jokes?'

Trevor loosened his tie, 'I thought They would help to calm your nerves.'

'Well, they didn't. Let's go.'

They crossed the road and walked casually into the shop. David went straight to look at the rings. Trevor was standing by the door. One assistant asked Trevor if she could help him. He told her he was waiting for his romantic friend. She went out the back. The other assistant was busy with David as he tried on rings. Trevor grabbed the Rolex, but there was a problem. The watch had a sprung wire fixed to it, and as he pulled, it set off an alarm. The two of them fled the scene as fast as they could and lost themselves in the crowds. After running for what seemed like miles they reached Sophia Gardens, and it looked like they had got away. They sat on a bench and removed their sunglasses. David blamed Trevor. 'You thought they just left a twenty grand Rolex sit by the door unguarded?'

Trevor grinned. 'I resemble that remark, and anyway, how was I to know a wire was connected to a microswitch in the display boxes out of sight. We better get a bus somewhere before we are recognised and taken to Cardiff castle to be executed.'

***

They eventually got back to The Tredegar Arms and laughed it off over a few pints of Brains. Trevor commented on David's beautiful ring. He never knew he wore one. David never knew he wore one either. It dawned on them what had happened, and they burst out laughing. David had been trying on expensive engagement rings in the shop and was wearing one when the alarm interrupted his thoughts of marriage to a non-existent Princess. Trevor was crying with laughter until he realised Maldwyn would be there soon. They could use the deposit to flee the country. Every time the door opened David shivered.

It was nine o'clock, and Maldwyn arrived to complete the deal. Trevor told him that David had some unfortunate news. David was shaking. *Why me*? He thought. 'Well, Mister Davies, I am afraid things didn't work out. Trevor messed it up.' Trevor handed over the deposit. Maldwyn never smiles.

'It's OK. No worries boys. Nice ring for a scumbag Dave, can I try it on?'

Trevor made a silly remark. 'It fits like a shoe.' Sold for two hundred and everybody was happy.

The boys walked home in the dark. David thought he heard footsteps behind them.

'Can you hear that Trev? He's following us.'

'David, he's a car dealer, not the Mafia.'

'Yes, you've already told me that, but it still didn't help me sleep. I just hope that gangster doesn't know where I live.'

'Funny you should say that Dave. He asked for a contact address, so I gave him yours. Oops, that was a tip of the slung.'

'Why mine? I'm going to Newport tomorrow, and I'm going to give him *your* address.'

'David, my little cockroach, you worry too much. Anyway, you wouldn't put a foot on that car lot.'

'OK, I'll ring him then.'

'You haven't got his number Dave, so I'll get him to ring you.'

'Don't you dare. I'm sick of the sight of you. We will have to wear disguises forever.'

'Dave, that's weird, wanting me to dress up for you. I'm not wearing stockings and suspenders.'

***

# Timepiece Crime

*Would it be such a terrible crime*
*If one could influence the flow of time?*
*To go back or forth, to descend or climb*
*To rewrite a poem so that it would rhyme*

*To put right a wrong that was a slip of the tongue*
*Or to plagiarise a song yet to be sung*
*To win an award that's undeserved*
*Or to mislay a gong that the Oscars reserved*

*Prevent an accident that shouldn't have been*
*Glimpse the future that should be unseen*
*Bring back a friend who shouldn't be dead*
*Is it such a sin to prolong life instead?*

Trefor Dylan Jones

2008

# Chapter 3

Jim Lockey and the Solemn Sun.

Jim Lockey and The Solemn Sun were performing at The Hullabaloo Festival at Burley Fields Lake, somewhere near Cheltenham, on Sunday the twenty-sixth of August 2012, and Trevor and David wanted to go. They didn't intend paying thirty pounds each for the weekend, so they had to find an alternative entrance. Trevor suggested using wire cutters, but they had to get to Cheltenham first.

David's parents ran two cars, but they went to work together in his dad's car, so the Vauxhall Cavalier sat in the drive all day, five days a week laying idle. Unfortunately, the festival took place over a weekend. David could drive, but his parents insisted he passed his driving test before they would let him loose on their car. His dad was insistent that at twenty-five David should be Married with five kids and living under someone else's roof. If people only knew the full extent of the pain caused by lazyitis!

The sisters, Linda and Sarah Collins visited The Tredegar Arms twice a week. Linda had a car, so Trevor had to persuade Linda into taking the four of them to the festival. He could talk the hind legs off a Welsh Mountain Goat. The girls always took part in the Tredegar quiz on Tuesday's, and guess what? It was Tuesday.

The Tredegar was ideal for a quiz as it consisted of one large room with plenty of tables and chairs. They also sold Brains, something David and Trevor lacked. There were seven teams. A team consisted of between two and five players. The girls sat on their own in a corner. Trevor waited until they had paid the one-pound quiz entry fee, before asking them if they needed expert help. Sarah was delighted, as larger teams had more chance of winning. It surprised her that the two boys wanted to join them, as she had never seen them playing in the quiz. When Linda spoke to Trevor, she always called him Bill. Reminders were futile.

The two sisters looked alike, although Linda was eighteen months older than Sarah. They were both average height, average weight, and according to Trevor, of less than average intellect. They lived in Beacons View, off the Heads of the Valleys Road, a five-minute drive from the pub.

The quiz consisted of two rounds of ten questions, five snippets of music and five picture puzzles. Each team had an answer sheet. They all sat around a table. Trevor (Bill) sat opposite Linda, and David sat opposite Sarah. The first round finished, and David thought they had done well.

There was a ten-minute break between rounds. This break was the ideal opportunity to coerce the girls into taking them to Cheltenham. Linda bought the drinks as *Bill* had lost his wallet, and David had left he's at home. Trevor asked David if he intended going to the festival. David said, ‘Of course, isn't everyone.’

Sarah asked, ‘What festival is this then?’

Trevor responded abruptly. ‘Oh, you wouldn't be interested.’

She tried again. ‘Come on Trev, where's the festival?’

‘It is The Hullabaloo Festival in Cheltenham. Jim Lockey will be there on Sunday. I suppose if the four of us went together, we might have some fun.’ Sarah asked Linda if she wanted to go to the festival, but Linda wasn't so keen on it. Trevor tried harder. ‘It won't cost much. We can get in without paying. The train fares are dear though. Dave and I were going to take loads of beer, but they won't let us on the train with it.’

The second round of the quiz began. Trevor was sure Sarah fancied him. David was sure Sarah fancied him. In fact, Sarah didn't fancy either of them, but she *did* fancy Jim Lockey.

It was a miracle, but they came third in the quiz. Third, even though Trevor insisted that an Instagram was a portable record player, and smallpox was a sexually transmitted disease. He couldn't be serious for a minute.

The conversation turned to the festival. Linda said she would drive there if they all shared the petrol money. Trevor asked if he could have his share now. She laughed, but David was sure Trevor wasn't joking. The trip was on, and the girls were to meet Bill and David at David's house on Sunday morning at nine o'clock. David would bring the sandwiches.

***

Trevor was late as usual. They still managed to get away by half past nine. Trevor had planned the route. Abergavenny, Monmouth, Ross-on-Wye, Gloucester, and Cheltenham. The journey would take two to three hours. David had forgotten the sandwiches but had brought the beer, and Trevor had to pay most of their share of the petrol as their *combined* money meant David only paid fifty-four pence. At least he did get the beer. The boys guarded the beer on the back seat. Linda asked Bill (Trevor) if he had any smoke. ‘Yes, thank you, Belinda.’

Trevor had a new one-liner. ‘Did you know Dave, that handsome ends with me, and ugly starts with U?’ The girls laughed. David said it wasn't original, and Trevor was a protagonist. Trevor laughed uncontrollably.

Sarah asked David, ‘What is a protagonist?’

‘A protagonist, my dear, is someone who copies another author without authorisation and uses that work as his own, by not crediting the original author, just as Trevor does.’

Trevor had tears in his eyes. ‘What a turd.’

Sarah looked confused. ‘Oh, right,’

Linda offered to give David driving lessons if he paid for the petrol. Trevor started laughing again.

***

There wasn't much traffic on Sunday mornings, so it was a comfortable journey. They agreed to stop in Ross-on-Wye as Sarah needed the loo, and Trevor was hungry. Linda had a rule, no eating in the car. Sex, drugs, and alcohol were okay, but no food as it was too messy.

They parked the car by the river and ate Linda’s cucumber sandwiches and bio yoghurts on the river bank.

David loved Ross-on-Wye. He read them a brief history lesson from a pamphlet, but no one was interested. ‘This small market town overlooks the River Wye. It is located between Hereford and Gloucester and is known as the gateway to the Wye Valley.' Trevor asked why? David ignored him. 'The rector was Doctor John Egerton. In 1782, William Gilpin published a book, Observations on the River Wye, the first illustrated tour guide in Britain.' The other three were bored-stiff and returned to the car to share a joint. At a quarter past eleven, they left Ross-on-Wye.

As they drove closer to Burley Fields Lake, the traffic increased. Everyone had taken Leckhampton Lane that leads to the car park. There were stewards everywhere, and the festival-goers paid on entry to the car park. Trevor directed Linda to Cripletts Lane, where they found a discreet way into the concert field. They parked the car nearby in the lane. The wire cutters were too small for barbed wire, so David held the wire apart while the rest of them wriggled their way through the gap. Unfortunately, David was now stuck on the wrong side, and the other three were debating who should help him. They played spoof to decide an outright loser. It took some time as Sarah had forgotten the rules. Linda lost and helped David who was not at all happy. 'Terrific. Nice to know you could find a little time in your busy schedules to help a friend in need.' Trevor's ingenious way into the festival impressed the girls, even though Linda had torn her multi-coloured blouse on the barbed wire.

It was bustling. There were musicians and jugglers everywhere they went. Long haired hippies with tents. Food and drink tents, and real ale. Trevor told them to keep their hands hidden, as it looked like they had been ink stamped on entry. They wandered around for ages with hands in their pockets. Linda bought them all a burger. David instructed everyone to use only one hand to eat. Trevor asked. 'How can we eat four burgers with one paw?' Linda laughed. Trevor nicked a programme that was poking out of a bloke's rucksack. The girls wanted to know when Jim Lockey was playing. Trevor checked out the weekend activities and music. 'Jim Lockey and The Solemn Sun will be playing at 9 pm on Saturday night on the main stage.' It was unfortunate that Saturday was yesterday. Linda wanted her burgers back. They still had fun. There was plenty of good music. David was contemplating becoming a hippy. He liked the Afghan coats and the idea of hanging out with Hare Krishna loony tunes. Trevor thought, *to wear a bloody great Afghan in the middle of summer was downright stupid, and the thought of spending all day chanting and eating lentils with a bunch of disturbed Hindus was unthinkable.* He danced around David singing, 'Hare Krishna, Hare Krishna, Hare Krishna, Hare Hare.' David was not impressed, as usual.

They spent the rest of the day walking about in the mud, drinking cans of lager, and smoking grass. They saw a few bands, and Trevor listened to poetry recitals in the green tent. Trevor said to David, 'Hanging is too good for poets; they should be drawn and quoted.'

Linda thought that was funny. 'You are a chameleon, Bill.'

Trevor wondered if she had meant that as a joke or if she was as stupid as she looked.

'Thank you Linda, and don't forget, where there's a pill there's a sway.'

David was still annoyed at having to wait three-quarters of an hour while the other three spoofed. 'Yes, your right Linda, he is a chameleon. A lizard, green and slimy.' He's also a consistent protagonist, he never invented *drawn and quoted*, it's an old one.'

'David, my little muddled goblin, a protagonist is one of the leading characters in a novel, just like we are. I, my little friend, am a green and slimy plagiarist.'

'Ah, you admit your guilt then, I rest my case.'

Linda was tired of the arguing. 'Stop bickering, being popular is the most important thing in the world. Now, let's go, or we'll never get home.'

David thought Linda spoke like Homer Simpson. Trevor thought she looked like him.

Trevor and David had been studying Homer for years. They were experts at recognising Homer doubles.

They spent the next twenty minutes trying to find the direction of the car. Eventually, they reached the barbed wire, and the whole scenario of getting to the other side repeated itself, except David insisted on going first.

They left around midnight and got back just after two. Trevor was curious, 'Where are we going next time?'

The girls answered in unison. 'Nowhere.'

Trevor slapped his head. 'Thank god for that.'

***

# After the Festival

(Field of Dreams)

A deserted field of half-eaten burgers
Crushed cans, plastic bottles, and bags
Bare twisted steel, once a performers stage
Twine and ropes, poles, and flags

Scavenging birds fighting for remnants
Of the Hullabaloo that's had its day
Now a muddy place of memories
A distant dream that's fading away

Trefor Dylan Jones
2012

# Chapter 4

The Steward's and The Llewellyn's

Trevor and David, were now both in their mid-twenties and were still single and living with their parents. An assortment of illegal occupations assured survival. They endeavoured to become lazier, wealthier, and infamous, but that was no easy task in South Wales. You had to work at it, and work was alien to the two Welshmen

David however, did get his lucky break. He visited Davies bookies of Merthyr, for his regular bet. The bookmakers were a small family run business. Mister Davies, a well-regarded man in the town, was a community-spirited sort who sang in the choir. Many residents preferred to use his shop on New Castle Street instead of William Hill's on the High Street, so it was always busy on a Saturday morning. David studied the Racing Post and picked out a treble. He preferred his horses in combinations. More luck than judgement. Just a feeling that if you pick three horses from three races at three courses, then *three* should have some relevance in the horse's names. So, Three of Hearts was running in the two thirty at Cheltenham, Third Degree, in the three o'clock at Haydock, and Lucky Number in the three thirty at Newbury. OK, so Lucky Number might not refer to three, but it's likely, as his dad always said, *third time lucky* when trying to coax David from his benevolent bed, and anyway, there were no more horses running that day with a suitable name.

Ten pounds win treble at SP. Three of Hearts came in at seven to one, so that was eighty pounds staked on Third Degree. There was half an hour between races. A cup of coffee and a few cigs, and bingo. Third Degree won at nine to two. David was shaking as he tried to figure out how much was going on the third race. It was easy, just ask Mary. What? Four hundred and forty on an outsider. A double would have netted him over four hundred quid. He might have had bet on one horse too many! More coffee. *One more cup of coffee for the road*, was incidentally, his favourite Bob Dylan song. This thirty-five minutes felt more like three hours. He paced up and down, muttering to himself.

And they're off. One pulls up with an injury. One refuses, and one falls, who brings down the favourite, leaving five. Two fences to go and the three in contention jumped safely over the last two fences. Spottiswood was leading by four lengths to the outsider, Lucky Number. Lucky Number gained ground but lost by a nose.

So close and yet so far away. David wished he had stayed in the pub. That was three pints' down the drain. He threw the betting slip in the overfull bin and waved goodbye to Mary. Just as he was opening the door to leave the bookies, there was an announcement. There was to be a steward's inquiry. David rushed to the bin and retrieved his betting slip. After a delay of about five minutes, he heard another announcement.

The stewards had disqualified number 4, Spottiswood for the jockey's improper use of the whip, and the winner confirmed to be number 3, Lucky Number. David went berserk. He had won, and Lucky Number was fourteen to one.

It's amazing how all the old punters had suddenly known him for years. They talked like they were part of his family and patted him on the back. 'Well done boyo, just like your father, you see. He knew his horses you see. When either of us won, we used to share the winnings you see.' (David's father had never seen the inside of a bookmaker's).

David went to collect his winnings. There wasn't a queue, who else would bet on an outsider in such a small field. *Oh, mighty shit, six thousand six hundred pounds*. David was on the verge of fainting. That makes you a millionaire in Merthyr. Mary gave him a cheque. 'I'm sorry David, but the firm is too small to keep that amount of cash here. A cheque is safer than cash anyway. Barclays bank is open until four o'clock on Saturdays, so if you hurry, you will catch them.' He ran across to Barclays, only to find Doris Hughes was about to lock the door. He begged her to cash his cheque. She couldn't refuse since he had caught her and John Griffiths shagging in the Tredegar Arms' toilets on New Year's Eve. John Griffiths was her husband's best friend!

David walked back to Dowlais singing *Take Me Home,* with his pocket bulging with

a massive wad of notes. He headed straight for Trevor's house. They went to the Tredegar, and David treated his friend to a mixed grill. They sat there talking for hours. Trevor said, 'David, you must be on the bookie's diet because you have put on ten pounds already. It would be more appropriate if you were named Bill as you have all the bills and Bill is short for William Hill.'

‘It would confuse Linda, Trev. Anyway, I like my name. My parents said they had a challenging time choosing a name for me. My dad wanted to name me David after Tommy David, the famous rugby legend who was born in Pontypridd, but my mum preferred Barry, as they had conceived me under the pier on Barry Island. I thought that was too much information really. They opted for David as they both agreed it sounded more masculine. I suppose they named you Trevor because it rhymed with Clever?’

‘No, It’s a long story. Mum’s uncle Trevor was the inspiration behind my name. Uncle Trevor died last year and by coincidence, on the first of April, my official birthday. He had been a Professor of Linguistics at the Centre for Language and Communication Research at Cardiff University. They thought his name might prove to be an incentive for their beloved child to learn and further his education. Don’t laugh.

Dylan Thomas was my mother’s childhood hero, and therefore my middle name had to be Dylan or Thomas. They plumped for Dylan, as there were ample Thomas’s in South Wales. They only told me recently. I thought I was named after Bob Dylan.’

‘You told me your birthday was March the thirty-first.’

‘I don’t want to be an April fool.’

‘Well, you are.’

‘Don’t tell anyone Dave, or your dead. After extensive research, I realised nothing important happened on the day I was born, only that the number one song in the U.S. was *Nothing’s Gonna Stop Us Now by Starship*.’

David had a thought, ‘My twin brother Alun died at birth, so I must be both alive and dead simultaneously.’

‘You are like Schrödinger's cat Dave.’

‘I’ve never met Schrödinger or his cat. I wouldn't forget a name like Schrödinger.’

***

August two thousand and thirteen. David was still an irregular member of the choir. A

concert was going to take place in France in a few weeks’ time, in a place called Huelgoat (pronounced Well-gwat) in Finistère, and David wanted to go. He intended to stay on for a few weeks after the sing-song to enjoy something other than rugby. It would be a birthday present to himself. He would be twenty-six later that month.

Trevor was jealous. He now wished he had joined the choir. A couple of members were always trying to get him to join, but he thought it was for old men and tossers like David.

The Collins sisters were always complaining that there should be no such thing as a Male Voice Choir, as it's sexist. They also liked to remind the men that in school the music teacher, Miss Evans, could never get boys to sing. The boys thought singing was tiresome and embarrassing, yet after leaving school, there was no choir for women or mixed genders. And when it came to trips abroad, women were not welcome. David couldn't imagine those girls singing in a choir anyway. They just liked to complain like their Mothers and Grandmothers before them.

The coach would be leaving midday on Friday the sixteenth, and they would reach France the next morning.

Apart from ten years rent arrears to mother, negotiated with massive discounts, David kept most of his winnings safe. He did not revisit the bookies for fear of losing it again.

However, Trevor managed to spend a small chunk of it on a couple of ounces of Skunk marijuana.

David spent his evenings studying French on his dad's computer. He hoped to spend a few weeks on his holidays, getting drunk and meeting lots of new friends. If he was lucky he might be able to persuade someone into putting him up for free, then more of his cash would be available for cheap cigarettes, tobacco, and wine, for his triumphant return home. He made a list of best sellers to buy. Old Holborn and Golden Virginia rolling tobacco. Benson and Hedges and Marlboro cigarettes. The cheapest wine money could buy, and a dozen bottles of single malt Scotch. If all went to plan, he should return with enough cheap liquor and fags to make a good profit.

The days passed slowly, and Trevor was itching to spend more of David's money before he went off gallivanting. He kept trying to combine their resources, but David was having none of it. "Dave, my little Welsh goldmine, you always loved that word combine.'

'Well, I don't no more.'

'Anymore, David.'

'Well, I don't anymore Trevor. You are trying to rob me as usual.'

'David, my little anteater, if it had not been for that *combination* in the bookies, you would still be a poor miners son.'

'My dad was not a miner, but you lad, act like a minor. I'm surprised you didn't want to show me that trick where a wad of notes spectacularly changes into Somerfield vouchers.'

'Give us the wad, and I'll show you it.'

'What do you take me for, an idiot?'

‘Yes.’

The day arrived, and David agreed to return with a magnum of Champagne like Formula One driver's waste hosing down the spectators. Trevor said this was why there were no Jewish Formula One drivers. David left to meet the coach. He boarded the coach with Dai, and they were off to France. At twenty-five, he was the baby of the choir, and spent the journey sleeping and drinking, and feeling unwell.

After a few comfort stops they reached Plymouth. David had been to Plymouth before, but would rather forget it. Dai had never visited the city. David pointed out to him that Plymouth was the Capital of Cornwall. Dai had always thought that accolade went to Truro, but as his years progressed he realised his memory was fading because David was often putting him right on the facts.

The ferry didn't sail until ten, so David and Dai had most of the evening to explore the city. They didn't need to go far. They found a small pub near the ferry, The Kings Head, A free house, frequented by the Marines stationed nearby. David reminded himself not to mention Brains, as that could scupper their plans. After combining their cash at Dai’s expense, they had an enjoyable time gambling on a strange game that hangs from the ceiling of the bar. They drunk plenty of Bass and enjoyed the company of the Marines and locals alike. David was in tears when several of the locals gathered and hummed the Welsh National Anthem to send them off with. They would have missed the ferry, but for a bunch of good-hearted Marines who escorted them into the ferry terminal to the amazement of the rest of the choir. Finding the cabins proved impossible, so they slept in the bar. The rest, as Trevor would say, is history. Sorry, a mystery.

***

# Fourteen

Roll two dice and when the dice stop
Add the numbers rolled, the numbers on top

Now add them to the numbers on the bottom of the dice
The total my friend is fourteen to be precise

Trefor Dylan Jones 2018

# Seventeen

Think of a number between one and eleven
Now add to that the number, seven

Add four to your number new
Then subtract from that number, two

Subtract your original number, mate
Now add to your new number, eight

# Chapter 5

## Bread of Heaven, Food for Thought

No such luck for Trevor now that David's gone to fulfil his dreams, Trevor suffered from boredom and his mind wandered. He spent several days looking at the computer, trying to figure out what it meant to be Welsh. National identity must imply more than speaking with a funny accent and wearing a daffodil and having a dragon on their flag. Only two other countries have a dragon on their flag, Bhutan, and Malta.

What Wales did have was the world's best National Anthem, Mae Hen Wlad Fy Nhadau. A rousing, boisterous, dramatic song that turns grown men into crying Taffy babies.

Written by Evan James and his son, James James. Both were residents of Pontypridd. Coincidentally, Cornwall and Brittany have adopted the tune for their own National

Anthems. David will be sure to think everyone is singing it for his benefit.

There's more, The NHS, devised in 1948 by Aneurin Bevan from Tredegar. Since 2007, prescriptions in Wales have been free for everyone. Gareth Bale, the world's best and most expensive footballer. Wales has more rugby legends than the rest of the Home Nations put together. And as for Oscar-winning actors, the list is endless. Sir Anthony Hopkins, Catherine Zeta-Jones, and Christian Bale for starters. Poor old Richard Burton never won an Oscar but was nominated seven times!

What else? Tommy Cooper. *Tommy Cooper,* I hear you cry, *surely, he's a cockney?* No, he's from Caerphilly, and don't forget the cheese. Dylan Thomas. The Royal Mint. Snowdonia, and Stonehenge! Yes, the stones used to build Stonehenge came all the way from Wales

There was one thing Welsh that embarrassed Trevor, Welsh Rarebit. Could someone invent a new Welsh dish that didn't involve leeks or cheese? Impossible. The English are famous for their Full English Breakfast and Beef Wellington, the Scots for their Haggis and Aberdeen Rowie, the Irish for their Irish Stew and Black Pudding, the French for everything, and Wales? Well, Welsh Rarebit! Trevor never considered cheese on toast as a national succulent dish. In fact, it was a joke that the English would remind the Welsh about at every occasion. Imagine hundreds of Welsh rugby enthusiasts singing their hearts out, 'feed me till I want no more', and they were referring to cheese on toast. The French eating cheese on toast was unthinkable. The mind boggles!

OK, it was time for the cheese jokes, like what cheese is made backwards? Edam. How do you approach an angry Welsh cheese? Caerphilly. 'What do you call the Gouda spiritual leader? Cheeses of Nazareth. Trevor must stop dreaming and get full-time employment. He will ask Giovanni about a job at the ice cream parlour. Even the Italian's are famous for their ice cream.

Bread of Heaven. Is that food for thought? What about becoming a chef? His distant companion David would make a good chef. He would enjoy *combining* the ingredients.

Trevor will become a cuisine recipe and menu designer, and travel the world instructing famous chefs on how to prepare his latest dish. For starters, we have a creamy, cheesy leek and mustard soup served with chunks of fresh cheese-and-onion bread. For the main course, we have prepared a generous portion of melted farmhouse Caerphilly with mustard seeds, on a bed of clay oven toasted Bara Brith speckled bread, topped with a sprig of fresh rosemary. That sounds better than leek soup and cheese on toast or Welsh Rarebit.

What is Rarebit? Where is that Oxford dictionary? He read aloud.

'Late 18th-century alteration of rabbit in Welsh rabbit; the reason for the term rabbit is unknown.' Now, the Welsh might be stupid, but what the hell does a rabbit have to do with cheese on toast?

Now for the perfect conclusion to your special meal. My light lemon cheesecake with a shortbread crust and lemon sauce has a mousse consistency. It cleanses the palette and is lighter than bubbles.

Trevor thought that food was poetry. He intends to write poems about recipes. Yes, he will become the first recipe poet laureate. It was always satisfying to see the specials board in pubs. Menus can entice people to eat. Even simple dishes can sound great and cost a small fortune. Now you *could* say bangers and mash, but a menu designer would say a trio of Cumberland Sausages served with pan cooked chutney & leek mashed potatoes and topped with a red wine gravy.

It was late, and Trevor was hungry. His mother always told him it was unhealthy to eat late at night. Trevor didn't believe it. If having a midnight snack was not healthy, then why do fridges have lights in them? And how do you know they go out when the fridge door closed?

A reality check was in order. Trevor's father always told him, stick to what you know. So, he did nothing.

***

Trevor had grown into a smart, handsome young man. Clean shaven, with short black hair. He thought he resembled David Beckham but was alone in that assumption. He courted Mary, who worked at the bookmakers. An attractive lass, but very straight-laced and would not tolerate any nonsense such as robbery. Trevor's excuse was that it was the redistribution of wealth. He fancied himself as a modern-day Robin Hood. Mary was too self-righteous. In fact, they didn't even like one another. She thought stealing from the Welsh rich was wrong. He thought taking money from the Welsh poor to fund a lavish lifestyle for a tweed-suited bookmaker was daylight robbery. His socialist tendencies were being revealed.

Trevor dressed well and often wore a suit and tie. He felt comfortable in it, and anyway, it was a tradition in South Wales. It was normal to wear a suit to the pub, but the times are changing. Incidentally, that was Trevor's favourite Bob Dylan song.

He took Mary to the cinema once a week. They both enjoyed comedies, but her preference was for romantics.

Fortunately, the Vue cinema in Merthyr offered Hobson's choice. The Victoria cinema had long since closed. They would follow the film with a drink or two in the Tredegar Arms in Dowlais. Mary had a small car, which helped them get away from Dowlais. They would often take a day trip to Abergavenny to climb the *Sugar Loaf* and have a meal somewhere. Sometimes they would go to Swansea and walk along the beach, or watch the football if Swansea were playing at home. If Swansea won, they would have a shag in the car while waiting at the traffic lights! Trevor always said, 'Mary, be mental with me,' and she was.

They both attended his grandfather's funeral. Grandad had taught him his trade. It was a well-attended funeral. He had been a well-liked man. Funerals were always notable events in the valleys. Everyone knew everyone.

No job, and still living at home in his mid-twenties. A bank or Post Office job would be ideal. Politics was Trevor's pet interest. He would often discuss local issues with his councillor friends in the Tredegar. He considered standing as a councillor, but lazyitis intervened yet again. Mary gave him an ultimatum. At least look for a job, or it's over. It was over!

Was this the right time to take driving lessons? David could drive, after a fashion. David never did take his driving test. He saw it this way, if you can drive, why would you take a driving test? He had a point.

The choir returned minus David. Trevor received a letter from him in the first week of September. He intended to stay a while longer as he was enjoying Huelgoat and had made a few friends. His French and the weather were dismal. He worked part-time in a Hotel, and this entitled him to cheap accommodation and food if it was available. He still had plenty of money and was busy looking for an investment.

Trevor replied, passing on the sad news about his grandad, and describing in detail how best to use David's money. Trevor needed a couple of grand as his stake money for an exciting new project. He wanted to become a professional writer. The idea was to write a poetic cookbook, and they would be stinking rich in no time.

David sent a reply. He ignored Trevor's brilliant idea. He was going to invest his money in a small property and was combing the area looking for something suitable. He was also annoyed at not receiving a Birthday card from Trevor. He intended telling everyone that Trevor was born on April the first and not March the thirty-first.

***

Trevor carried on practising his chess openings and his three chords on the guitar. He missed taking Mary out. When Trevor went out on his own, he had to pay.

He wanted a pet, but his parents wouldn't have another animal in the house! Who would look after it? Trevor couldn't help due to his illness. Surely, they would allow him a cat or a canary. Yes, a canary would be good. He could teach a canary to speak Welsh or to bark like a dog. It would be a *Canary Wharf*. Yes, they are sure to let him have a canary. He will name it David. He asked his mum. 'No Trevor. Your father and I do not have the time to look after a canary.'

'Mum, I am twenty-five years old. I can look after it.'

'No.'

Later that month Trevor received another letter from David, informing him that he had invested his winnings in a bar in Plouyé (pronounced Plue-E-A). Trevor wondered If David needed a hand in the till. Oops. A hand with the till.

The previous owner was an old woman who lived in the one room upstairs. When she found it too arduous getting up and down the stairs, she went to stay with her son and daughter-in-law in Landeleau, a nearby village. He picked it up for a song. David insisted that reading The Racing Post had developed his purveyance skills. He knew some long words but didn't quite know where to use them.

Now, his new bar was a far cry from the plush Grand Lac Hotel, where he was staying, but then most bars were. The thing about bars in France, he wrote, is that old ladies owned most of them. They lived there, and when they felt like it, opened the doors to the public. There was at least one in every village, and they sold a variety of goods. These places were like corner shops with the added luxury of incorporating a café and bar.

He chose to name his new pub, Penydarren, in memory of Trevor's grandfather who lived in Pen-y-Darren and had died recently. Trevor was impressed with the thoughtfulness of his friend. The bar had no real ale, and anyway, the three locals only drunk Pastis (an aniseed-flavoured liqueur and aperitif served in tiny glasses). They would take over an hour to drink a glass. Sometimes they would sit by the fire and not drink at all.

David was sure that he'd be speaking fluent French in a few more weeks. He was getting free French lessons from an American woman, Angie, who owned a small bar in Huelgoat. She had lived there for some years with her English husband, Jim, but he had now run off to Belgium with Odette, a second-hand furniture dealer. Angie was in her mid-thirties, slightly overweight with curly blond hair and not bad looking. The weird and wonderful thing about her place was the illegal drugs she sold openly. Even some of the Gendarme would arrive after midnight and join in the fun, drinking, and smoking cannabis, and keeping things under control!

David helped in her bar occasionally. Angie had said he could move in with her. David rejected that idea because of her insane husband who could return from Belgium at any time. He was a physical trainer and might not approve. David had worked part-time at the Swan in Abergavenny until he lost his lift, so he was not a novice in the art of serving alcohol or drinking it.

David was excited about his new venture, but buying a property in France, when you couldn't speak the lingo was not easy. He enrolled Angie to help with the process, and she was more than willing. Everyone he met said she was more than willing.

***

Trevor spent the next few months still learning to play chess, believing it would help with his strategic thinking. He thought of joining the local chess club but didn't fancy walking to Merthyr every week. They also charged a joining fee, so he played on his dad's computer. His pseudo-name was Trevorsky.

Trevorsky never excelled at chess but did enjoy writing poetry. *Recipe for Disaster* was his latest poem. It had been a long time forming but was nearing completion. Mixing ingredients in his Mother's kitchen for the sake of a poem was a mammoth task for a small brain, but he felt that the poem had to make culinary sense.

He hadn't heard from David for a while, so decided to phone him. It was nearing Christmas, and he wanted his Champagne. He waited until his parents were out, as they forbid him making long distance calls. David supplied him with the phone number of Le Grand Lac Hotel, where he spent most of his time working or drinking.

It amused Trevor when a female French accent answered the phone with, 'Le Grand Lac Hotel, Puis-je vous aider?' He asked for David the Welshman. She yelled, 'David (pronounced da-vid), Anglais Monsieur sur la téléphonie.' Not good news. David said he had been too embarrassed to write, as he guessed Trevor would tell everyone in Merthyr about the tragedy. As if! The fire started after a late-night drinking session. Luckily, David had not been there when it caught fire. He had stayed in the spare room of a local alcoholic's house, which had a real bed in it. The problem was the open fire. A log somehow rolled out and set light to a table, which in turn set light to everything else. A stray cat may have been the culprit.

The news got worse for David. No insurance. David always thought it was for losers!

Therc had been very little stock. Some bottles of cheap wine, Coreff, and Pastis. The upstairs room survived most of the damage, but the bar was ashes and stone. David told Trevor he desperately needed his help but knew he would have to lure him over. He needed him to stay awhile so he could activate his cunning plan, but more about that later! He knew Trevor enjoyed their combined scams but would refrain from using the word *combine*. David proposed they did a job to raise the cash needed. He could sneak Trevor into his room at Le Grand Lac Hotel. There was also the fact that they would be able to nick as much food, drink, and fags as they needed.

Trevor never liked the French. He thought the language was

feminine, and grandad said that during the war, they were as useful as an ashtray on a motorbike.

Trevor reluctantly agreed to go, but only for a few days. It wouldn't do any harm to learn a few choice words. Back to the computer. First things first, 'I would like two beers please'. 'Je voudrais deux bières, s'il vous plait'. Easy. That should be enough to get by on.

Trevor's dad could speak French. Trevor asked him to jot down a few useful phrases. Mum would lend him a few bob for life's little luxuries. Trevor will be off to Plymouth, bound for Penydarren on a cold December day. He was going to enjoy his first Christmas abroad.

***

# Recipe for Disaster

(Welsh pork stuffed with Prunes)

One large fillet of Welsh pork, boned
Eighty grammes of cooked prunes, stoned
One medium carrot, sliced
One large potato, diced
Fifty grammes of almonds, flaked
One small tin of navy beans, baked
A pinch of salt, pepper, and, spice
Fifty grammes of washed basmati rice

Spread the meat flat, season and spice
Mix the prunes with veg, almonds and rice
Lay the stuffing along the middle of the meat
Roll up and secure with string or with cleat
Place on a tray, the whole combined mix
Preheat the oven to gas mark six
One and a half hours in the oven is fine
Cooked to perfection and eaten with wine

Trefor Dylan Jones 2013

# Chapter 6

Brian Ferry

Trevor prepared for his journey to foreign lands. Just a week to pack and tie up any loose ends, which reminded him. Linda Collins spoke to him in the Tredegar last night. He was sure she fancied him now and no doubt he will lure her into his bed before he leaves for France. He might write a love poem for her. Women love poetry. How about robbing a Shakespeare sonnet and rearranging the words? That would be easier than starting from scratch, and Shakespeare would surely approve.

He decided he would write her an original poem dedicated to her, but he would see how the date goes first. He thought of giving her a leaving present like Roses. No, not roses the flowers, Roses the chocolates. Trevor loved Roses. She might drive him to France. Um. Would she get on his nerves too much?

Linda rang at three that afternoon and said she would meet him in the Tredegar at around eight and he can take her somewhere posh. An ideal opportunity to persuade her into going to France. She must have forgiven him for messing up the Quiz and the festival, etc. Should he take his passport with him just to prove his name isn't Bill? Trevor dressed up in his best suit and tie, polished his shoes and arrived at a little after eight. He waited over an hour in the so-called *cosy seat* by the dart board. Why people would want to call a seat next to a dartboard cosy was beyond Trevor's imagination.

Linda didn't turn up, so Trevor and a few of the lads spent the evening playing the Austin Powers fruit machine. Gareth, the landlord, had barred Trevor from playing the machine because he always won, so his mates would gather around it while he sat in a corner conveying the expected outcome. Trevor knew that fruit machines were not random. This one worked on the high-low principle. For example, if an eleven was showing on reel one, you had to choose a higher or lower number between one and twelve. The manufacturers pre-set the reel for high (twelve) as most punters would obviously go low, so they would lose. Trevor could remember all the predetermined numbers; therefore, Brains was free for the evening.

He never did get Linda into his bed, and she hadn't forgiven him. Trevor was sure it was a wind-up, she hated him. He will not be writing a poem for her now, nor will he be buying her Roses. Well, he could still get the Roses.

It was time to learn the guitar. It had been lying around for months. It was a superior classical guitar, the most expensive guitar in Strings and Things in Newport. He nicked it together with an electronic tuner, and a book entitled *Play Like Chet Atkins*. That book must have been new old stock! He remembered an old one-liner. It's easier to Tuna fish than tune a guitar unless it's a Bass.

He sat in his room practising the three chords he had taught himself. C, F, and G7. Someone told him that with a capo he would be able to play anything using just those three chords. He hadn't considered busking before but decided to have a go. David wasn't there to laugh at him. He sorted out twelve simple songs, enough to last the afternoon. The shoppers would love him. A dog would have helped. All buskers had a dog. That would have been ideal. Better still, a white stick and dark glasses. He had kept the dark glasses he stole from 'The Pound Shop' in Merthyr that they used in the botched Rolex job. Now, where will he get a white stick? He rummaged around dad's shed. There were fishing rods, but they had lots of little hook things tied to them. That won't do. Bingo! He found a fish holding net on a long white aluminium pole. Just one little snap dislocated the pole. Dad will never miss it. He prefers golf anyway. He also found an old, long black coat that stunk of fish.

He put on the coat and dark glasses and wandered off to Merthyr, tapping his white stick on the cobbles and stone walls. He looked like a blind hobo, a bit like a smelly, untidy, Ray Charles. No one would recognise him now.

He stood outside the camera shop on Merthyr High Street on a cold Friday afternoon, singing songs in the key of C. Trevor thought he sounded quite good. A cross between Bob Dylan and Stephen Hawkin. He collected six pounds and seventy-four pence, plus three foreign coins. That equates to two pints and a sticky bun. Quite a few of those punters said,

'Hello Trev' as they passed. What's a capo anyway? It sounds like an Italian gangster.

***

Trevor's mum drove him to Plymouth port in good time to board the morning ferry to Roscoff. She had supplied him with money for his fare and food, and a suitcase full of clean clothes. It was as if she was glad to see the back of him! The ferry terminal was an old three-storey building with an escalator and lift that took you to the departure lounge. There was a bureau de change at the terminal counter, so he bought himself some Euros and a ticket. He kept his British money in his wallet, and the Euro's in his inside pocket. He knew all about pickpockets! The spacious departure lounge was furnished with round tables, surrounded by fixed seats. There was a little cafeteria, where he bought a cup of tea. Trevor loved tea.

The terminal was almost empty. Trevor thought he had made a mistake. He was insecure. Once he had found the outside balcony and had a cigarette, he could see the boat was in the dock. What a relief. A quick smoke and he came back in to find people were queuing to board. Foot passengers accessed the ship via a long, partially uncovered walk which involved negotiating stairs and slopes, while carrying oversized suitcases. Well, he did, everyone else had cases on wheels that make a thundering noise as they echo through the tunnel.

As he boarded the ship, several good-looking French girls were awaiting his arrival. They all dressed in red, white, and blue uniforms. *That's nice*, he thought, *they dress in British colours to help us feel comfortable.*

David was going to pick him up from Roscoff, in his old English plated Cortina. David had told him that English registered cars were best because the gendarmes were not likely to pull them over due to the paperwork involved. So most English registered vehicles had no tax or insurance and bald tyres. The police never stopped them. So, if you owned an English plated car, you could drink what you liked, drive where and how you wanted, and not bother with tax or insurance. David guessed that before long all cars in France would have English plates.

The Armorique was Brittany Ferries flagship. Trevor had already read all the information about the ship and knew where to go. He found his way to deck seven, where 'Le Bar' was, and found a quiet corner. The sea was calm. There were few passengers, and the outer decks were empty. It was too cold and windy. He sat at the bar inventing new phrases. If the ship was called Bryan, would it be a Bryan Ferry, and Who's going to pay the ferryman if we sink?

His father had taught him a few French terms, and he was adamant he would use them. He wanted a coffee and a slice of cake. A few practice runs, and he was ready. He approached the bar, where a large stern-faced redheaded Madame was serving. Here goes then, he thought.

'Bonjour Madame. Un café et un votre laid.' She looked angry and replied.

'So, you think I am ugly? You are not exactly a Monet yourself.'

Trevor blushed. He should have known his dad would do something like this. 'I am so sorry about that,' he blurts out. 'I speak only a little French. Your English is good.' She served him a coffee, black in a cup designed for a mouse. *Anyway*, he thought, *she is ugly. She looks like a dwarf in cheap clothing*. He wasn't sure he'd got that right.

The ferry was scheduled to arrive at three o'clock, and the hours felt like days.

Trevor had been warned that only one pack of cigarettes were available from the bar at the reduced price of four Euros. He had no intention of buying his fags from the boutique at the more expensive rate, so he conceived a plan. Trevor bought one pack from the poker-faced bald man, and then when the bald man went to collect glasses, he bought one pack from the stern-faced redheaded Madame. He then used his ink marker to re-invent his face with an instant moustache and put on the now famous dark glasses, then bought another pack from the bemused bald man and another from the giggling redhead. It wasn't until he used the loo that he realised the ink marker was green! If he found a mop, he could change his hairstyle and get two more packs, but was that overdoing it? He wanted some more but was afraid the two muppets would recognise him.

*It's strange*, he thought, *the passengers are English, and the staff are French. How much easier it would be if the staff were English, or if the passengers were French, curious*!
It was nearing three o'clock, and everyone was preparing to get off the ship. It was another half an hour before the passengers were finally allowed to leave. *Why the delay?*

***

The port of Roscoff looked so much better than Plymouth. Plymouth port was old and grey. This port had a modern look, with plenty of free parking. Trevor couldn't imagine how the ferry stayed afloat with all those cars, lorries, and coaches on board.

It was a short walk to the ferry café, where David would be waiting for him. No sign of David. A cup of coffee and a bun would go down well. An Algerian looking chap wearing a red beanie stood at the counter. Trevor decided on just the coffee. 'Un café.'

'Yes sir, large or small, black, or white, and do you require sugar?' came back the reply.

'Oh, you speak English. Great. Large white please, with one sugar. You speak excellent English.'

'Thank you, sir. A few of us French have the gift to converse in a language that we hear all day every day while doing our simple jobs. My name is Aissa, and I am here to serve you. Please take a seat, and I will bring your coffee over, Bwana.'

Trevor sat down and pondered. *Was that man being sarcastic*? Aissa brought the coffee over and they had a chat. 'So where are you headed, Englishman?'

'I'm meeting my friend here and we are going to a place called Plouyé and then to a place called Huelgoat.'

'Ah yes, I know Huelgoat. A lady-friend of mine, Martine, is going there sometime around Christmas to unveil a plaque celebrating the forest.'

'Oh, maybe I'll meet her. I'm Welsh by the way, not English.'

'Welsh, what does that mean? Are you interbred?'

'No, not really, although I like the odd sandwich.'

Aissa looked puzzled as he walked back to the counter. Trevor was about to drink his coffee when in rushed a small skinny Frenchman wearing what looked like tights and a beret and leather waistcoat. He ran around in circles shouting out a tsunami of words. An elderly English couple sat at the next table. They must have been English as only the English wore Manchester United scarves at that age. They must have spoken French as they knew what was afoot.

Trevor asked the Englishman what the problem was. 'A car has hit the back of a van, and a small carton fell out and broke open. It was in transit from England to Brest medical centre and contained several dangerous species of scorpion, but all is well, they have all been recovered.'

'That's a shame,' said Trevor. 'One of those would have made a nice gift to post to my dad!'

David arrived and entered the café flanked by two bleary-eyed policemen. They had guns. Trevor hadn't seen a policeman with a gun before. They sat in a corner, and the big man took coffee over to them. David had not seen Trevor yet, and Trevor was happy to let them get on with it. David signed and dated several copies of paperwork, and the police left. Trevor wandered over to David, who was swearing under his breath. 'What's the fuss all about Dave?'

David smiled and said, 'Oh, I'm sorry I'm late, I had a slight problem with my brakes and bumped into a van. They are prosecuting me for no tax or insurance, and for having bald tyres! I must not drive the car. I should get a letter in the post explaining everything. I think we had better be off before it gets dark. The lights don't work either. I'm just glad they didn't breathalyse me. I hope you got your cigarettes from behind the bar as I said. They don't care how many packets you buy at once as long as you are polite.'

'I know that, David. I'm not stupid.' Trevor felt stupid.

Trevor said goodbye to the English couple and apologised for his friend. They waited outside for the gendarme to go before they left in the strange looking car that David should not be driving. It was freezing and raining. 'What make of car is this Dave? I've never seen anything like it.'

'I'm told it's a hybrid. I know the back half is a mark one Cortina because it has *ban the bomb* rear lights. I think the front is a Renault. It was cheap.'

‘I bet it was, you soft tosser.’ The heater didn't work. Trevor had to hold the door handle, as the door did not stay closed unaided. This task was difficult as it meant Trevor had to hold his beer, and the joint they shared, with one hand. He asked David if he knew the way. ‘You can't go wrong It's a straight road. Simples.’

There were loads of roundabouts, and everyone drove around them the wrong way. Trevor thought this must be dangerous, but fortunately, there was little traffic. They spent the journey from Roscoff to Morlaix discussing the work needed to get the bar up and running. They had to raise a few grand for repairs, and another grand for stock. Oh, and enough for a car. They would have to do a job! They both agreed not to rob a jeweller. David suggested cars.

‘Not if there anything like the one you’re driving Dave, I suggest antiques.’ David wanted to rob a Museum. Trevor said he liked paintings.

‘The trouble with paintings Trev is that they are hard to sell.’

‘I don't want to nick paintings, Dave. I was just saying I like paintings.’

David wanted to build a small stage in the corner of the bar. The local musicians would come and play for free. They loved to play their accordions and a weird instrument like a flute that resembled a daffodil. The singers are atrocious, but who was he to complain.

David drove his clapped-out car slowly to Morlaix, where they visited The Giant (pronounced G ant) for a quick meal. It consisted of a little meat on a big bone, with fries and salad. David had done the talking, and it didn't sound like he had got very far with his French as they were served two meals each. It didn’t matter. They were hungry.

The Giant was a massive hypermarket. They sold everything from matches to mattresses. They had a quick wander around and replenished their beer supplies. David topped up his mobile phone. They filled up with diesel, or gas-oil as the French like to call it and got on their way.

The drive took them through the Breton countryside, and it was not long before David had to admit that he was off-course. He should have turned left at the television beacon. 'David, you pillock. Who said, we can't get lost, it's a straight road? Off-course. Of course your off-course you prat.'

'I'm not lost, we are just going an unusual way. We'll soon be back on track.'

'Unusual way! Back on track! Off-course. You're lost, you dim-witted Welsh clown.'

They drove around for ages until they were back on the right road.

Trevor noticed several old abandoned houses. David told him how family members would club together to buy a property. When it came to selling them, there would be disagreements, or someone had moved or died, and the property remained unsold. 'They still haven't updated the laws. Change is hard to come by in France Trev.

Trevor slapped his head. Not because he is a masochist. He always did this when he had thought of something funny and original, and that wasn't often. 'If change is hard to come by in France, Dave, I won't be using their vending machines.'

Trevor didn't understand why he did not see Roscoff. He saw lots of Plymouth when he travelled to the Plymouth port, but when he got to Roscoff, Roscoff was missing! David ignored him.

It took another hour to reach their destination, the bar named Penydarren. Trevor's left hand had formed part of the door handle. He had a job to pry it away.

***

## All Dressed Up with Nowhere to Go

Sitting anxiously watching the phone
Desperate to hear the ringing tone
She promised to call. I'm sure she will
Come on Linda, swallow the pill

It's half past three and time is telling
Not one called, not even selling
Then the phone rings, 'Hello Bill
It's Linda here, are we going for a meal

Her soft voice sounds nervously excited
She can meet me tonight. I'm delighted
Around about eight in The Tredegar
Five hours to wait and I'm feeling eager

Stop playing chess and shower and change
Smoke some weed and feeling strange
Get to The Tredegar and have a drink
Where is Linda, the missing link?

Sitting, staring at the front door
Mesmerised by the carpet pattern no more
Time presses on, and she doesn't show

And I'm all dressed up with nowhere to go

Trefor Dylan Jones 2013

# Chapter 7

Aardvark and Clotted Cream.

Plouyé is a small commune in the Finistère department of Brittany in north-western France. It has a population of 676. The village, bordered to the south by the River Elez, and to the west by the River Alder, is not more than a few miles from Huelgoat. There is a bar/shop, a school, a pretty Church, a library, and about eighty small stone houses. The rest of the population live on the outskirts.

The wreck of a building, renamed Penydarren, once had two windows and a front door. They entered to find a lot of debris and a dangerous looking staircase. There was no electricity, so David lit the candles. The ceiling was not complete, but sturdy wooden beams saved most of it. The roof was a little damaged. Trevor looked for another door. 'Where's the stage going?'

David looked around, 'In that corner Trev. I realise there's not much room.'

'You're not kidding grasshopper. These people must be tiny. I thought the place would be full of ash and smell of burnt wood.'

'It's been very windy of late Trev.'

The building stood on a small plot with only an outside loo. The houses on either side had survived any damage. The woodwork and windows took most of the blunt. Penydarren will need two windows and a front door with some urgency, then a replacement bar, stools, and tables, and redecorating. Oh, and stock. The pavement had room for a couple of tables and chairs. David assured Trevor that it was normal to put tables and chairs outside. 'They would never allow that in Merthyr, Dave. Elf and Stacey would put a stop to that.'

On the other side of the wide road was a large communal car park and a grassed leisure area where the dogs came to shit. Trevor thought, *why a car park in a place with so few cars, and plenty of room to park on the street?* Around the corner was a large square with a plush looking Maire office flying a Breton flag. At the front gate stood two stone pillars with weird looking stone heads perched on top of them. The building looked impressive and appeared to be extravagantly large when considering the size of the village. Opposite the Mairie office was a bar, The Sports Bar. A dismal looking place.

There were more stray dogs and cats than people on the streets! It was cold and raining. The sky was colourful, and Trevor could see a faint rainbow. 'What's the beer like Dave?'

'There is no beer as such, just lager and girly drinks. When the pub is up and running, I plan to import Brains. I believe these poor deprived people deserve a proper drink. What have you been up to Trev?'

Trevor had to think. ‘Oh, not much. I've written a few poems, taught myself chess, taught myself to play the guitar, shagged Mary, and was stood-up by Linda. I don't blame her either. She didn't like me biting my nails, so I put my shoes back on.’

It was early evening and time for a drink. ‘Come on Dave. I think that’s enough work for one day. We wouldn’t want our lazyitis to start playing up, would we now? Blow the candles out, lock the door and let's ramble on.’

‘What door?’

He took him around the corner to The Sports Bar. ‘One thing you must not forget Trev. If you go into a bar, do not ask the barman if he has Brains. Trust me on this one. In fact, when it comes to drinking anything, you are better off drinking your own blood. If you want a cup of tea, forget it. The French find putting a tea bag in hot water a truly ambitious task. Drink coffee, and ask for 'grand café au lait,’ (pronounced, gron caf-A o'lay) or you will get a thimble full of sickly thick black stuff. And listen to this. You must make do with girls’ lager in small glasses like English girls use. French men drink like girls. Lager, wine, or Pastis in small glasses. Trevor grunted, ‘I’m going home.’

‘Don’t worry Trev, there’s a guy in Huelgoat who sells cider and a pub in Carnoet that sell their own beer.’ They walked towards The Sports Bar, and as David passed the Maire’s office, he looked over and put his thumb up. Trevor ignored him.

***

As they set foot in the bar, Trevor noticed that it looked more like a small supermarket. There was so much stuff that it was hard negotiating the route to the bar. An overweight, red-faced, long-haired man in his sixties welcomed them. He was sitting behind the bar staring into a bright red tanning lamp. 'Daved halo, how tis morning you is.'

'Fine, thank you Wim. I would like to introduce my friend Trevor to you. He is going to help me with the bar.'

'Twevor halo.'

'Halo Wimp.' They all shook hands.

'Wim supplies the locals with tanning lamps to help speed up the cultivation of grass. He keeps one to use as a heater, and that's why his face is red. He speaks decent English but somehow rearranges the words.'

Trevor was busy looking at all the stuff in this place. Some of the food appeared dangerously old. Cheeses and large sausages hung up behind the bar, and orange boxes, full of what may be bread were laying everywhere. All weird and strange shapes and sizes.

Wim passed them two Coreff lagers, but no money changed hands. David said Wim was Dutch and then he lit up a cigarette. Trevor looked at him, 'Isn't smoking in pubs banned in France?' David and Wim laughed. They sat at the small bar on the only two stools in the place and chatted for many hours and with many drinks. None of which had been paid for. David couldn't remember if he blew the candles out before they left Penydarren.

'With the gale force winds that blow through that place, I don't think you have to concern yourself with that.'

To Trevor's annoyance, David started singing *Take me home*. Wim joined in, except Wim was singing a version of the country song *Tak me om county wose*. David was singing a completely different song, written by a Canadian for The London Welsh Choir! It was difficult to tell the difference!

The morning had arrived, and they were getting tired. Strange looking people wandered in and bought loaves of that stale looking bread and croissants that a thin man wearing a blood-stained apron had delivered earlier. Trevor grimaced, 'That bread looks stale and why are the buns shaped like boomerangs?'

'That is Breton bread Trev, and it is not stale.'

'OK, I just hope that's beetroot on his apron.'

David gives Trevor another lecture. 'Brittany is definitely different to the rest of France Trev. For one thing, these people think the Welsh, Irish and Scots are just like them. Apparently, it has something to do with being Celt's. They have their Breton language that sounds just like Welsh, Gaelic or Scottish, and they are very proud of it, but hardly anyone speaks it! Just like the Welsh, Irish and Scottish! It's a pity they don't speak English, just like the Welsh, Irish and Scottish? Oh, and they drive much safer when they are drunk. There is no such thing as fresh milk, so forget your corn flakes. In fact, you can forget breakfast altogether. For breakfast, they eat sticky buns with chocolate bits in them and drink water. Not from a tap. They buy it. For lunch, they all sit at one big table like a re-enactment of The Last Supper. They all smoke while they eat, and they drink gallons of cheap wine. They eat small portions of rabbit food, followed by the little meat on the big bone with couscous or skinny chips. They finish off with a Cornetto. Old Giovanni would turn in his grave. When the wine runs out, a waitress just brings more. They eat and drink for about two and a half hours; before one by one, they drift away back to work. If they are not in the café, they sit in a bar eating cheese on toast like Welsh Rarebit. They call it croque-Monsieur and slap a slice of wafer thin ham on top.'

‘Oh no, not like Welsh rarebit?’

‘Yes.’

‘I’m going home Dave. These people are cycle paths.’

‘Cycle paths? Oh yea, very funny.’

It was time to have another look at Penydarren and then get some sleep. As they left, Wim shouted ‘Euro sexy sex.’ David had forgotten his wallet. He had a small amount of change and offered to combine it with Trevor's. Trevor paid. And silly Trevor had thought this all-night session was on the house.

***

As they turned the corner, they noticed what a lovely bright morning it was, but still cold and raining. A few people walked around. There were old women with dyed hair and bright red lipstick and little old men with sticks. They were all wearing scarves and carrying loaves of unwrapped bread. David shook hands with all and sundry. Trevor had to shake hands with some of them. David kissed some of the women on the cheeks. The church bells started to ring. The church looked like something from a spaghetti western. Trevor expected to see Clint Eastwood walk out of the church, with two smoking guns and wearing a blanket.

On entering Penydarren, a scruffy looking black cat with a bald patch on one side scattered away. Trevor said, ‘If he was looking for milk, he's in the wrong country.’ David lit the candles he had in glass jars. Trevor saw that the bar floor must have taken most of the brunt, as it was missing and only dirt remained. ‘A new floor will cost a small fortune, Dave.’

‘There is nothing wrong with the floor Trev. It was always like that.’

A small sink sat behind the burnt-out bar, but there was no water, David was resilient. He had an old metal watering can that he kept filled with water. They could at least splash their faces.

‘Tomorrow Trev, we will go to Huelgoat (pronounced well-gwat) to eat some real food and meet some interesting people. You are going to love this place.’

‘Dave, let's get one thing straight, I don't intend staying any longer than I have to.’

‘Of course not, Trev.’

Trevor had one last concern. ‘Where do we get our weed, grasshopper?’

‘No problem. I have a friend up the road who grows his own. He supplies the whole country, well almost. It's good stuff, and Angie makes nice cakes with it.’

‘You have been busy Dave. How such a reserved Welsh boy has sussed so much out is amazing, I must congratulate you.’

‘Thanks, Trev.’ They lit a couple of cigarettes and talked for a while about David's new friends.

‘I even made friends with the local Mayor. He's half English. He wants to meet you sometime. He has some clever ideas and being the Mayor; he can do anything he likes. Imagine if you were a Mayor. With your political bent, you would like that, wouldn't you Trev?’

‘No. I’m going home.’

‘Was you surprised when I won all that money on the gee-gees Trev?’

‘Not really, you were born a professional gambler Dave. I did quite well with Creosote.’

Creosote. Was that on the flat?’

‘Yes, but it’s just as good over fences.’

They climbed up the rickety staircase, each holding a candle jar. ‘This isn't a room David. It's an attic.’

'All upstairs rooms in France are attics with tiny windows in the roof, which is normal. At least it's mostly boarded.' There were cobwebs everywhere. A small window in the roof would have let light in, but it was too dirty to be of any use.

They crashed out on beds of old fancy cushions and blankets. If it hadn't been for the copious amounts of Coreff, sleeping in this cold, damp, uncomfortable place would be difficult. The floor felt unstable, Trevor was sure they would wake up downstairs.

'Goodnight Dave boy.'

'Goodnight Trev boy.'

The chilly wind blew through the roof, but sleep they did.

***

It was sometime in the afternoon when David's sweet dreams were abruptly interrupted by a little man shaking the blankets and shouting. 'David and you friends, come to my houses for food.' (The French can't say the word *house*) David introduced him as Pierre, a friendly local man who he met in Huelgoat. They rubbed their eyes and went downstairs. There have had been intermittent showers all morning that pounded the roof tiles, but they managed to sleep through most of it. They went to Pierre's houses for some grub.

Pierre, a skinny man with a bent back, lived just around the corner from Penydarren in a small, sparse stone building, with a little back garden. The front had no garden. Downstairs was one large room, like most houses in this part of France. One side was the kitchen area, the other the living space. Six old wooden chairs surrounded a big oblong table which had a giant globe stood in the centre of it. David said,

‘Pierre knows every capital city in the world but has never been to any of them, but he loves his globe.’

Trevor remarked, ‘That globe must mean the world to him.’

The wood burner was a big cylinder with a flat top, on which stood a pan used to boil water for the coffee or to cook a meal. A stack of logs stood each side of it. There was no cooker. A fancy, old-fashioned sideboard took up most of the room. It was so cluttered with rubbish, that papers and chess pieces had fallen off it onto the floor. Trevor noticed the incomplete chess set on it. He couldn't imagine Pierre playing chess. Was it worth giving him a game? He thought not. There were two small bedrooms upstairs. David had slept in one of them on many occasions after drinking too much Pastis.

He lived two doors from the library, but Trevor didn't think he would have much use for that either.

‘So, what do you do for a living Pierre?’ Trevor asked.

David laughed. It seemed like every time Trevor spoke, David laughed.

‘In Finistère, work is a secret. It's like the black market in Wales, except everyone's in it unless they work in the Mayor's building. Pierre left the house to use the toilet.

Trevor smiled, ‘We do have that in common, outside toilets.’

‘There is no outside toilet Trev. These old houses have no toilet, inside or out.’

Pierre returned, and the three of them smoked a little dope before Pierre prepared the food. Bread and Camembert. The bread looked like something he saw in Wim's bar, but it tasted great. Crusty on the outside and soft and sweet on the inside. Trevor was enjoying it.

‘It looks like sliced Aardvark and clotted cream.’

‘You won't find any clotted cream in France, Trev’.

Trevor joked, ‘I'm on a fish diet, and I've lost six squid already.’

Trevor lit up a cigarette. The ashtray was spilling over with dog ends, so he took it to the bin to empty it, but the bin was overflowing. Pierre took the ashtray from him and tipped it on the floor.

‘It OK, I broom soon floor.’ David rolled another joint to enhance the Breton music Pierre loved so much. It certainly needed enhancing. It was weird and sounded dreadful. The record player looked like an old Dansette from the fifties. David had been learning about this type of music. ‘It is called Kan ha diskan (translated as call and response) and is the most common music in Brittany. They sing it to strange dance music. The lead singer is the kaner, and another singer is the diskaner. The kaner sings a phrase, and the diskaner sings the last few lines with the kaner. A kan ha diskan lasts from 5 minutes to half an hour.’ Trevor took little interest. They all giggled about nothing, and Pierre kept talking French to David. Neither of them knew what he was saying, and this just made them chuckle even more. He made some coffee, and it tasted awful.

They left early for a good night's sleep before a day of reckoning.

***

# Blow the Candle Out, Let's Ramble On

The blades of grass are sheltered by the dew
As the morning opens yawning, creeping through
The sun takes its place in Heavens well
And silhouettes the peace down here in hell

So turn a leaf, don't you look back now
The world beyond is there for you to plough
Today informs me that we should be gone
So blow the candle out, let's ramble on

The seagulls praise the wind and lend a claw
To the baptised rocks resting on the shore
The tide is anchored to the shifting sand
Sweeping long lost seashells from the land

So turn a leaf, don't you look back now
The world is yours and is calling for your plough
Today informs me that we should be gone
So blow the candle out, let's ramble on

Trefor Dylan Jones 1998

# Chapter 8

Le Grand Lac Hotel.

They were up early and set off to Huelgoat in that dodgy car. David wanted to leave it parked up somewhere until he got it sorted but he considered himself too old for hitchhiking. The plan was to sit somewhere and brainstorm ideas to raise money to get the bar up and running.

David had gathered a lot of information about Huelgoat, famed for those huge boulders, the forest, and cannabis cakes.

Huelgoat was a small traditional Breton town, dominated by the town square, an open public space found in the heart of most populated places in Brittany. The square was the approved space for community gatherings and the outdoor Saturday market. It was also an ideal spot to buy or sell illegals.

Small shops and bars surrounded the centrally located town square. Many of the shops lay decking outside on the road to accommodate tables and chairs. Even in the winter, people sat alfresco to eat and drink. Every other shop was a bar. That was another contrast between Brittany and Wales, or in fact anywhere. There was a plumber's shop that sold beer, and two bakeries that sold beer. Three creperies and two hotels that sold beer. Even the bookmaker come coffee shop sold beer. There were two restaurants and a café that sold beer. There was a tobacconist that sold beer, and believe it or not, five bars that sold beer. All of this in one square. The fuel store did not sell beer, but some of the locals drunk Ethanol. The residents boycotted the two estate agents as they did not sell beer. Who would want to move from a small town with so many bars in it? There was a Haberdashery that sold materials and accessories for clothes, and a flower shop, a couple of banks, and a post office.

They drove around the town. A vast forest, infested by massive boulders, surrounded Huelgoat. It looked strange, like something Tolkien had put there. Le Grand Lac Hotel sat around the corner from the square opposite the lake. A pretty lake used by children, who could rent a pedalo or a kayak from Claude Laffont, a little old man who sat outside a small shed beside the lake, whatever the weather. David liked Huelgoat because he could buy food that resembled something like home.

The Buccaneer belonged to a Cornish-man and his French wife. They sold Cornish pasties and fish and chips. An English woman and her French husband owned the Fork and Shovel. They were famous for their pizzas and steaks. Trevor renamed it The Shit and Shovel. The Giraffe, owned by an Englishman and his French partner (gays), sold ice cream much as you would buy in Giovanni's. Angie, the American, run a small bar called Angie's Bar, and she sold cannabis cakes, a sort of food.

David had made friends with many of the residents of Huelgoat. People shouted 'ça va', or 'salut David', from across the road, and the men stopped him to shake hands. The women dressed in colourful skirts and scarves, apart from the older ones who wore black. They all dyed their hair, young and old. Many of the men used walking sticks and looked older than they were. Trevor saw that no one wore a necklace of garlic or onions, nor did they wear blue and white stripes with berets. Most were walking up and down clutching baguettes, shaking hands and kissing. To think, he lived in Merthyr all those years and hardly knew a soul.

***

David took Trevor to Le Grand Lac Hotel, a charming, roomy hotel made from white Breton stone. As they entered, the first thing to catch Trevor's eye was a massive chandelier. David described it as a Venetian-glass beaded iron, hand-made classic within an antiqued silver frame. Trevor paid little interest as it was too big and awkward to take away. The spacious hotel lobby and bar was furnished with lots of tables, chairs, and sofas. The floor was French marble with marble pillars scattered around. The walls were red and adorned with French paintings with people wearing traditional Breton clothing. The long copper-topped bar doubled as the registration desk and extended the width of the room. In the right corner was a broad winding staircase leading to the sixteen guest rooms upstairs, and a few more reserved for the joint owners. To the left was the smart glass-walled restaurant, where they partook of an early lunch. A runny lamb stew with funny green bits, and crusty bread. You could sit in the restaurant and watch the world go by, just like you see in old

American films. In fact, it reminded Trevor of the hotel in the film Casablanca.

Two French men (not gays) owned Le Grand Lac Hotel and spoke excellent English, as they had worked in London for many years as Chefs in The Hilton. They were excellent musicians and entertained the clientele by playing their guitars in the evening. David and Trevor finished their meal and sat in the bar with a drink and prepared for their brainstorm.

In walked a broad bearded man and approached David. ‘Gooday Dave, it'll freeze your fucking bollocks off out there. What's the John Dory mate? David nodded and introduced Trevor to Patrick. An Australian, of Irish descent, who was wearing flip-flops, a tee shirt, and a pair of old ripped jeans. He had a bar in Cleden-Poher that opened in the evenings. During the daylight hours, he was the local trader of stolen property. ‘Gooday Trev, what the fuck are you doing here. Come to fuck about with Dave's burnt out house?’

Trevor smiled and offered Patrick a seat. He gestured to the barman to bring a drink. ‘I'm fucking parched. You got any shit man, Angie's only got cake.’ David handed him a piece of silver paper. ‘Cheers Dave, I'd better hit the frog and toad. Got to see some prick about some antique swords.’ He drank his beer and stomped out. He somehow reminded Trevor of Bluto, Popeye’s adversary.

As they gathered their thoughts about the future of the bar, there was another interruption. One of the co-owners, Jean-Jacques (pronounced Jhon-Jhack) had come to introduce himself to Trevor. They all shook hands. Jean-Jacques was in his fifties. Quite tall, and slim, with a thin moustache. He wore a dark suit and an open shirt. He was very excited. On Saturday, a celebrity would be coming to stay at Le Grand

Lac Hotel. Madame Martine Rousseau, a legendary French actress and singer, would be staying at the hotel. She was to formally open *The Christmas Plaque* which describes the history of the boulders in Huelgoat forest. Her entourage would arrive at 6 pm, on Saturday, December the twenty-first, 2013. Trevor was intrigued. ‘What is a Christmas plaque, and how do you open it?’ There was no reply. Jean-Jacques asked David and Trevor if they wanted to earn a small fortune, with the emphases on small, helping to prepare for her arrival.

‘You can both have rooms and food from now, Tuesday, until after she leaves sometime early next week, in return for some simple cleaning and bar work.’

Before they bit his hand off, they negotiated an amount of beer to be inclusive. They shook hands, and the world was a beautiful place.

At last, no interruptions for a while. Now that they had rooms and food and beer for a while, it would be easy to concentrate on earning decent money. Trevor enquired as to how much was in the till at the end of the week, but David insisted he couldn't rob this place. Jean-Jacques had been kind to him. David had always been a softy, and Trevor never did understand how David got out of that bookies with his winnings intact.

‘What about the bookies, Dave?’

‘No good. The only gambling in these parts is a few Euros on the Pari-mutuel which few people understand, let alone use. That's why the bookmaker sells beer.’

They agreed that it might mean going to Paris and nicking a miniature painting from the Louvre, or something like that. Trevor put his thinking cap on, and they had another beer. Trevor had a plan. ‘We can't go to Paris while we are staying here, so why don't we get drunk and worry about it next week.

Remember my saying. Never do today, what you can do tomorrow, and never do tomorrow, what someone else can do today.' David agreed.

***

Another cold December day, another adventure. Jean-Jacques was sitting at the bar having a thimble of coffee. David and Trevor walked in and greeted him. He bought them a thimble of coffee before offering them the chance to turn down a job. 'David, my friend, are you and Trevor capable of cleaning the chandelier. It will be a delicate job that requires patience and concentration.' Trevor was at once reminded of an 'Only Fools and Horses' episode that ended with disastrous results. 'Of course, you can do it in situ.'

David looked puzzled. 'Oh, I think we would rather do it here.'

'I mean you don't have to remove the chandelier, so it is simple enough. All you need do is clean the crystal prisms and beads with a damp cloth. The bigger pieces should be wiped over very gently as they are irreplaceable.'

Trevor asked. 'How much will we be paid.'

'Nothing, but I will not throw you out to die in the freezing cold until next week as previously promised.'

'OK. We will service your chandelier first thing tomorrow morning.'

'You sure Trev? It sounds a bit daunting to me.'

'David, my little ray of sunshine, it is a doddle.'

***

The two chandelier cleaners were up and about early, and after a small breakfast and two or three coffee's they set to work.

There was a tall step ladder available, and Trevor was there to keep it steady. Everything had been carefully prepared for them. A large bucket of soapy water and some fine cotton cloths. The cleaner had lent them triangular signs with French and English versions of *No admittance* printed on them in bright red ink. They placed these by the main door and by the stairs and the entrance to the restaurant. A blanket covered the floor to soak up any dripping water that might cause the ladder to slip.

David stood on the top of the ladder while Trevor soaked the cloths in the warm soapy water. David, perched precariously on the ladder, was cleaning the glass droplets on the chandelier. He had almost finished. Trevor was holding the ladder with one hand while drinking a lager with the other. They were discussing why Montgomery Burns employed Homer Simpson in Sector 7G at the Springfield Nuclear Power Plant.

'That plant, Trev, is installed with two Fissionator 1952 Slow-Fission Reactors and despite hundreds of safety violations, it's still operational. It's been near to meltdown loads of times and blown up once. It doesn't make sense to give such an important job to an idiot.'

David wasn't concentrating on what he was doing, and as he cleaned the big glass ball on the bottom of the chandelier, it became unhooked and smashed onto the marble floor. It's in bits.

'Oh, shit Dave, how did that happen.' Trevor blamed David. David accused Trevor of wobbling the ladder. They would have to replace the ball, and quickly. Jean-Jacques was due to inspect their work soon.

They hurried off into the square to find a replacement. The nearest thing to a glass ball they could see was a Christmas decoration. A fancy bauble made of a shatterproof material that resembled glass. Not a hand-made, antique, Venetian-glass globe, but it was 70cm, and Jean-Jacques would never notice the difference from a distance, especially as he always looks down, hoping to come across a lost euro. They rushed back breathless and fitted the five Euro ball. Trevor thought that was expensive for a crap Christmas decoration.

They cleaned up the floor, put the ladder and cleaning kit away and sat at the bar.

Jean-Jacques arrived and thanked them for an excellent job done. He bought them both a drink and walked away whistling *Hymne a l'Amour*.

'Blimey Trev, what would we have done if it wasn't Christmas? I suppose we could have found a clairvoyant somewhere and nicked her crystal ball.'

'No Dave, she would have known it was us, she's clairvoyant.'

'Very funny Trev, I wonder if those crystal balls really work. What would you do if you had a crystal ball Trev?'

'I would sit down very carefully Dave.'

They spent the rest of the day telling each other jokes about balls.

'What would Angie get if she were holding two balls, Trev?'

'Your undivided attention.'

'What's the most expensive meat in France, Trev?'

'Deer balls.'

‘Who is Beckham's favourite politician, Dave?’

‘Ed Balls, and you don’t look anything like David Beckham. You look more like Donald Duck.’

***

For the next few days, they did a little cleaning and painting, then got drunk.

It was now Friday, and Friday is a heavy drinking day in Huelgoat. They plan to visit some of the most curious pubs in the town. When they had finished the morning's work, it was time to rock and roll.

They went on a tour to some of the drinking joints in Huelgoat. Trevor refused to combine the cash. They had their first drink in the bookmakers called Chez Camille. It was a combination of café, bookmakers, nightclub, shop, and a pub. Many traders were like this, neither one thing nor the other. In common with the norm, it resembled an English working man's café, with cheap metal tables and stools, a service bar, and a considerable array of cigarettes. Not much gambling went on there, mostly elderly women with a spare couple of Euros. Even the French couldn't understand the Pari-mutuel. David said it was like the tote. It was a busy place, but most were drinking coffee. A door led to the unused Grotto nightclub. It had once been a busy nightclub, opening at midnight and closing when the last drinker left. Stories had been going around about the activities in the club, but now the deserted grotto was just a cold, damp room, but for the cobwebs covering the imitation boulders.

The next stop was the plumbing shop, where they had a drink with Michelle, the blind man who was the owner. A simple shop that sold plumbing accessories and camping gas and beer! As they were leaving, David told Trevor about the time the blind man got in trouble.

'According to Pierre. A few years ago, when Michelle could see a little better, he had left the shop to post a letter, and not being able to see very well, tried to post it in a Muslim woman's eyes. She thought he was a terrorist and screamed like hell. A local priest comforted her until a policeman arrived and charged the blind man with assault. Since then the full burqa has been banned in France.'

'I think you'll find your little friend was having you on Dave.'

Trevor insisted on a beer in the bakery, because, 'I've never drunk a beer in a bakery before, and anyway, they knead the dough.'

David smirked, 'What? and you have drunk beer in a plumbing shop!' They had a quick beer in the bakery and a strange episode it was with men coming in to buy loaves of bread. It was interesting to see how many men came out to buy bread. Some would come in groups of up to six or seven, drink a beer or two and then leave with a loaf. 'Now you see why the men insist on helping their wives by going to the bakery for them Trev.'

They then walked around the corner to the Shit and Shovel, as Trevor liked to call it. The Fork and Shovel was a rock and roll bar. On the left was the bar, its walls covered with signed pictures of mostly British rock stars, and there were guitars on the ceiling. On the right was the restaurant. The boys shared a giant pizza and a jug of lager while listening to a loud rendition of *Dark Side of the Moon*. The owners were a husband and wife team and had only been there a few weeks. He was French and loved motorbikes and loud music while she was a northern English girl with a strong Manchester accent. When she spoke French, her accent changed to a soft Riviera accent. Strange. She pranced around the restaurant singing out of tune while her hubby served beer and sang *in* tune. A tall, thin man wearing a white chef's costume wriggled about behind the serving hatch, smoking a cigar, and making pizzas.

A man was re-wiring the electricity meter. He turned his head to David, 'Hello David, how are you.'

'Hi Mick, I'm fine. What's up, replacing old wiring?'

'No, I have to run the cables from the other side of the meter. EDF always connect the cables to the wrong side, and then the owners must pay for electricity. Diverting the cables is a full-time job around these parts.

'Oh, right.' David didn't understand electrics. They finished their pizzas and moved on.

They met all sorts of strange and friendly people, but none stranger than Angie. Her pub looked like it was once a hotel. A double fronted building with huge dirty glass windows. Trevor wiped an area of the left window and could see old furniture and lamps hanging from the ceiling. The right window was curtained, but he could make out the images of people, and it was very noisy. The front door opened into the bar where dozens of people were sitting around listening to modern jazz and eating cakes. There were all kinds of antiques scattered around. An opening to the left had a sign above that read, 'Fair and Square Antique's'. It led to what resembled an overfull auction room. While in Angie's bar, after Trevor had coerced a few Euros from everyone with his Stand-up Monty, they had a breakthrough in their quest to finance David's bar.

Angie talked non-stop, and she knew all the local gossip. Trevor noticed that she had American flags painted on her fingernails. The bar was small and intimate. It resembled an American museum. The French liked her, as did the English and Irish communities. Everyone came here for her cake, full of homegrown grass or American cannabis. Even one of the local Maires had a regular takeaway!

Angie was ranting on as usual about all and sundry when Trevor overheard her discussing Madame Rousseau. ‘She's coming downtown tomorrow and will be checking in at the Lac. She may even sing a few songs, accompanied by Jean-Jacques and Christian. Rumour has it that she wears a small purse around her neck that holds the diamonds left to her by her deceased shipping magnate husband. Some say she bumped him off. She is bringing her hairdresser who-’ Trevor intervened, ‘David, get this bird a drink, she must be perched. What are these diamonds, Angie?’

‘Oh, she has six small diamonds, which are worth thousands of bucks, that her old man left her. He also left her a yacht and several houses.’

Trevor grabbed David, and they went outside to talk. ‘This is it, Dave. We will have to verify the dates and times at the Lac.’

David was excited ‘Let's go.’

***

They rushed back to the Lac. Jean-Jacques was at the bar instructing a young girl to clean all the glasses once again. There was no time to spare. Trevor shook hands with Jean-Jacques, another strange habit the French had. They shook hands or kissed everybody they met, even if they know them well. They only did this the first time you saw someone on that day. Some French men disliked the habit as their wives would fathom if they had already been to the bar. If he didn't shake hands or kiss the proprietor, then he was a lying scumbag who had been out drinking all day. This situation didn't often arise these days as most blokes knew the rules and would happily shake hands again to avoid bloodshed. Once you knew a woman, you kissed her on both cheeks. Sometimes you didn't have to know her. It depended on the woman and the situation. It could be complicated. The French spent all their time shaking hands and kissing before lunch, so there wasn't much time left to do anything else. After lunch, they were too intoxicated to do anything, and therefore they did nothing.

They sat down for a drink with Jean-Jacques. Jean-Jacques could not do anything until he had a beer, not even a little chat. It was hard to bring up the subject of diamonds without it sounding strange, so Trevor had an idea. Reverse psychology. Another thing he learnt from his late grandfather. He began. 'So, Are you all ready for tomorrow evening, Jean-Jacques?'

Jean-Jacques was still watching the girl behind the bar. 'Yes, we are almost there Trevor.' He shouted something in French to the girl and then turned to Trevor. Now for the punch line.

Trevor directed the question that would start the debate. 'So, what is she like then, this woman?'

Jean-Jacques looked stunned at Trevor. 'She is a lazy little bitch that spends all day on her iPhone.'

Trevor was not expecting that reply. He tried again. 'But she is rich, isn't she?'

'Rich! If she's had her grubby little fingers in my cash drawer! Why? Have you heard something? I will sack her now!'

Trevor realised they are at cross purposes. ‘No, not her, I mean Madame Rousseau. Is she wealthy and flamboyant?’

Jean-Jacques paused and then answered. ‘In France, she is like your Madonna. No, Madonna's American. She is famous like your Lady Di. No, she's dead. Ah, if she were a man, she would be comparable to... Is there anyone famous in England?’

‘No,’ replies Trevor, ‘but we have Tom Jones in Wales. He is famous, but I don't like him myself. He's from Pontypridd.’

David couldn't stand anymore. ‘Does she have any diamonds?’

Trevor shook his head, wondering what his grandfather would think of that. *Talk about giving the game away.*

Jean-Jacques went on. ‘Oh, the infamous purse of six diamonds worn around her neck. She removes them only when she sleeps. Some say she can feel her late husband's hand when she touches the purse, and others say she killed him off for his money and doesn't feel anything.

‘Her manager contacted us about her suite and security. My partner Christian assured her that her diamonds would be safer here than in the Louvre. Trevor now thought that the small painting might be a better bet.

‘Incidentally boys, Christian calls you Welsh men *sheep shaggers*, how funny is that?’

‘Not very,’ said David.

Now it was Trevor’s turn. He had never been diplomatic. ‘Christian said a halfwit gave you a piece of his mind, and you kept it cos anything’s better than nothing. How funny is that?’

Jean-Jacques walked off.

Trevor *borrowed* a torch from a bicycle that was leaning against the Lac's outside wall, and they had a stroll into the forest and collected six small stones, which they wrapped in silver paper. All guesswork, but a similar weight would delay D-day when she would miss her husband's legacy if by chance they happened to get their mitts on them. They had an early night. They will need to have their wits about them tomorrow.

***

# Le Grand Lac Hotel

*Dance my love beneath the shimmering chandelier*
*We will drink the calmness of the atmosphere*
*Explore the fragrance of the midnight air*
*Linger a while on the winding stair*
*Love as we only would dare*
*With extravagant flair*
*Our emotions bare*
*Without a care*
*A night fair*

Trefor Dylan Jones
2013

# Chapter 9

Diamonds are for Trevor.

Saturday was market day in Huelgoat, and the hotel was always busy on market days. Stalls filled every space available in the square, selling exotic food and spices. There were also clothes, hats, and umbrellas for sale. You could buy a whole cooked chicken or pork slices with couscous. There were games and fair rides for the children. The square came alive on Saturdays. The bars were bursting with folk drinking coffee or alcohol and all the people were milling around chatting with each other. It was an exciting day for locals and tourists alike. It would be hectic, despite the rain.

Madame Rousseau was due that evening. After completing their daily chores, Trevor and David sat down for a discussion about relieving her of her jewels. It would be their biggest job, and precise execution was paramount. David thought that it would be an impossible task to get them from her suite, as Jean-Jacques said he had installed extra locks and security. Trevor had other ideas. 'If she invited me in for a nightcap or hat, I would not have to force entry.' That was possible for Trevor, who was quite handsome, clean, and tidy on a good day. He could also charm the pants off a politician, but then who couldn't? An alternative would be to execute the single-handed clasp twist, while David distracted her telling her stories from the valleys. Of course, she would have to be able to understand English. Not too difficult to perform the twist if he could get close enough. He would have to guess what type of clasp anchored the chain. It was likely to be a spring ring clasp or a lobster claw. A toggle clasp would be unlikely, as it is not very secure. A lobster claw with safety chain was the best bet, and quite easy to remove.

They decided to opt for this method. The best time to execute it would be on Sunday evening. After a long journey, she would be going to bed early that evening. All they had to do was to stay sober until the following evening when she would be enjoying the Huelgoat hospitality. David tried a Trevor type quip, 'Do you think you can pull it off? Get it, pull it off.'

'Yes Dave, but can you stay sober until we're in possession of the jewels?'

'Of course I can, stupid. *Pull it off.* Tell the truth, it was a good one wasn't it Trev?'

'No.'

They had a few hours left to go over Madame Rousseau's schedule. No doubt after arriving at six, she would be having a meal and an early night. She had four assistants that included her hairdresser, manager, makeup artist, and bodyguard. Jean-Jacques' partner, Christian, had already sealed off part of the restaurant. She would then go to her suite. He had allocated six rooms to them. Five en-suite bedrooms, and a bedroom he had rearranged for use as a lounge for their privacy.

She would be up early Sunday morning, and after eating sticky buns, she would leave to do the plaque unveiling thing. Lunch follows at the Maire's request so she will not return to the Lac until around five. They knew all this owing to their cunning detective work and the fact that there was an article in Le Telegramme, the local paper, describing her schedule. Sunday evening is when she would relax. Having done her work.

David asked, 'What is plan B?'

'Plan B, my little misfit was the band headed by Ben Drew, who sang *She Said*.'

David looked confused, 'Ah, I get it, you mean the group called Plan B. OK, very amusing. Seriously though, when she misses her diamonds, she will call the police, and we will go to prison, where we will then be abused by famous DJ's and politicians.

Trevor assured him that the purse could be replaced around her neck or put back on her bedside table as quickly as he had removed it.

'She may never know until she decides to sell her rocks in ten years' time. By that time I will be in The Bahamas drinking Margarita's with a bevvy of gorgeous girls, and you will be in Penydarren drinking Pastis with a few smelly French-men.'

They agreed that from now on they would refer to the diamonds as the baby, as French walls have French ears that might understand French English. David wondered if it was all worth it.

As Wim was in Huelgoat, he called in to see the boys. 'Daved an Twevor, halo.'

David said, 'hello.'

Trevor said, 'halo.'

'For you two both, I buy beer, yes?'

They both said, 'no.'

Trevor told Wim that Welshmen cannot drink today, the twenty-first of December because of their religion. In the Northern Hemisphere, today is the first day of Winter and the shortest day of the year, and they can only drink coffee.

'North Hemisfir tis is not, tis Huelgoat. I buy beer.'

Trevor gave in. 'OK, just one.'

They had one beer with Wim before he left to re-open The Sports Bar.

They planned to be well behaved. Something to eat and an early night. It would be quiet there tonight, and there would not be any food served, except for Madame Rousseau. Jean-Jacques would no doubt want to close the bar early so that she could sleep.

Only a few hours remained to have a pasty in the Buccaneer before it was bedtime. They would spend all day tomorrow, relaxing without beer or drugs to distract them.

***

The Buccaneer was a small pub on the corner of the square run by a Cornish-man, Perran. He cooked English food, and the pub was popular with both the English and the French. Perran was married to a French woman. He had been in Huelgoat for fourteen years, and his children, a girl, and a boy were both born in France.

The pub resembled a small British pub with a polished mahogany bar, but no real ale. There were pictures of Cornish seaside towns all over the walls. The roof beams had beer mats advertising Cornish beer pinned to them. A mirror on the wall behind the bar had a giant pasty painted on it. There was an oversized book behind the bar entitled *The History of Cornwall.*

The pub wasn't busy. Just a French couple, sitting in a corner eating pasties. Perran was behind the bar. A short, balding, stocky man of about fifty. He introduced himself with, 'Woss on'.

David asked, 'Perran, do you come from Plymouth?'

'No, Cornwall stupid.'

'But Plymouth is in Cornwall.'

Perran gasped, 'Oh shit! I must ring my brother and let him know d'recly. He lives in Plymouth and thinks it is in Devon.'

David ordered two pasties while Trevor surveyed the place. Perran brought the pasties over to them. He even had tomato sauce. The pasties were massive. Perran said they were 'proper job' pasties. He said he was proud of his Cornish heritage and sold Cornish Cider from a village called Lerryn. David asked him if he were born in Lerryn.

'No son, I was born in Kent, but keep it to yourself. Brittany is one of the six Celtic nations, along with Cornwall and Wales, so if you want customers here, you have to be one of the six.'

The Welshmen loved conmen. 'Who are the other three nations then?'

'The six territories recognised as Celtic nations are Brittany (Breizh), Cornwall (Kernow), Wales (Cymru), Ireland (Éire), the Isle of Man (Mannin), and Scotland (Alba). When I first moved here, I had to choose a nation. It was a toss-up between Cornwall and The Isle of Man.'

Trevor asked, 'Why not Wales?'

Perran laughed uncontrollably.

His wife came in with a couple of carrier bags. A well-dressed woman who looked several years younger than him. David did the kissing thing, and she shook hands with Trevor. She had a short conversation with her husband in French, then disappeared out the back. Perran said, ‘She loves me for my book.’

David was impressed, ‘Oh, the big book all about Cornwall?’

‘No, my chequebook, Stupid.’ He sounded like Trevor. They had a few Lerryn cider's, a few more, and then fell asleep slumped at the bar. Perran woke them up, ‘I told you to be careful with that Lerryn cider.’ he said, although he didn't look too good himself.

Trevor found it difficult to lift his head, but managed and asked, ‘What's the time?’

‘Twenty past one. Do you want a drink?’

David went outside. He felt sick. Trevor followed. He had the worst headache ever.

‘We blew it,’ he said.

They strolled back to the Lac. As they approached, they heard singing and laughing. As they approached the open door, they could see crowds of people. Jean-Jacques and Christian were playing their guitars, and a woman was singing and dancing on a table. There was a table full of succulent food, everything from Scotch eggs to caviar. A waiter offered them a drink. It was hard for a Welshman to refuse. David helped himself to several profiteroles. He saw Patrick in a corner smoking a joint and joined him for a chinwag.

Trevor sat by himself nursing his headache. The singer looked over at him and shouted. ‘Qui est le bel homme?’

Someone helped her off the table, and she stumbled over to Trevor who was half asleep. She slumped herself on his lap and asked, 'Ce qui apporte une belle homme comme vous dans un endroit comme celui-ci?'

How could Trevor respond, and not sound like a prat? 'Bonjour Madame, I do not speak French.'

She smiled at him. 'Oh, the dear sweet thing is English. I think bonsoir would be proper at this hour. And who is this beautiful young man that God has delivered to me.' Their faces were almost touching. Her breath smelled of Cognac, and his of Lerryn Cider. She was attractive, and around thirty-five, he would suspect. She had blonde hair and blue eyes and was wearing a very low-cut dress. Huge breasts heaved into his chest. He looked down. There was an elegant necklace with a small purse dangling from it.

'Oh my God, it's her!' he spurted out loudly.

He jumped up suddenly, and she fell to the floor. She looked as if she had just been tossed out of a low flying helicopter. Trevor had blown a golden opportunity. 'Oh, I am so sorry madam. Let me help you.'

She muttered a string of French profanity's and picked herself up off the floor. 'Why did you do that? Bonjour would have done just fine.' She was about to return to the others.

Trevor had to think quickly. 'Please don't go. I like you.'

She looked at him with a wry smile. He felt like an idiot, but it was the first thing that came into his stupid head.

She started laughing. 'OK, but don't throw me on the floor again.' She came back and sat on his lap. 'What are you doing here Englishman?' He disliked being referred to as an Englishman, but he didn't want to say anything that might upset her.

‘I have come to France with my business partner, David, to refurbish a Hotel he has recently acquired.’ Fortunately, she could not see David, who remained slumped on the floor in the corner, drunk, and stoned, with the remnants of profiteroles and blueberries masking his good looks. He looked like a small child who had been set loose with a selection of crayons.

Trevor was happy with the way he bent the truth. He gazed into her eyes and leant towards her. His right hand behind her neck. He kissed her as he executed the single-handed clasp twist on a lobster claw with safety chain. Purse and chain fell gently into his suit jacket. *Would she notice?* It was surprising, but people didn't. Even if you removed a bulky wristwatch, the owner never noticed. Anyway, that was the theory.

It was effortless, as she had fallen asleep on Trevor's shoulder. He fondled for the purse that lay between them under his jacket. Christian, who was still playing the guitar, glanced over. He thought Trevor was touching her up while she slept. *That could not be normal*, he thought, *even for a sheep shagger.*

Trevor unclipped the purse and removed the diamonds. He then replaced the diamonds with the silver packet of stones and transferred them into his inside pocket. He now only had to reattach the purse to the chain. He did this while leaning her back and kissing her again passionately. There was a lot of fumbling. Christian could not believe his eyes.

Trevor then planted Madame on one of the sofa's in the lounge and wandered around, speaking to as many people as possible. That was another form of misdirection. Even though it was early morning, quite a few punters remained in the building. David had gone to bed. Everyone was sobering up and drinking coffee. The place was a mess. Trevor slipped away to his room. He was too tired to examine the diamonds and passed out.

***

Trevor woke up with a hangover and a tune in his head, *diamonds are forever*. It was a cold Sunday afternoon. He inspected the diamonds. They were bigger than he had imagined. There were six as expected, but who's counting. Not her he hoped! They would have to get them valued and plan a way to sell them. He had a shower and dressed, then hurried downstairs to find out if she had missed them.

There were several young employees collecting glasses, cleaning, and tidying. The place was in a mess. He sat on his favourite sofa to wait for David to arrive. On second thoughts, he decided it was best to get away from this place, so left a note behind the bar for David, saying he was going to the tabac and David was to meet him there.

He made his way to the tabac and sat in the corner away from inquisitive ears. A large man managed the tabac. He spoke no English and had a bad cough. It was no wonder. You couldn't see for smoke. This place looked like any other tabac. There was a counter with a vast collection of cigarettes on a display stand. The French had a wide choice when it came to buying cigarettes or tobacco. Next to the counter was a bar with several stools. Opposite that was a magazine rack. Most of the magazines had a video or CD or part of a plastic model attached to them. There were a few newspapers like Le Monde. Trevor drank a coffee. He was watching the door. Would two plainclothes policemen enter and arrest him? Would Jean-Jacques come running in screaming about his reputation in shatters? Would Madame's bodyguard beat him to a pulp, and then again, and again? Would the maid discover Madame's lifeless body in her bed, after dying from a broken heart? He didn't think so. None of this happened,

David arrived, looking like a green alien. He sat next to Trevor with his head in his hands. 'Oh well,' he said. 'I've always wanted to visit Paris. Are you sure they don't screw the paintings to the wall? Anyway, this will cheer you up. While I was pissed, I had the courage to let down one of Christian's tyres. That'll show him.' David knew nothing of the night's escapades. It might have been better if it stayed that way.

Trevor was too soft. He looked at David and smiled. 'Bore da, my little Welsh friend, it is a done deed my little sparrow.' He then whispered into David's ear. 'Diamonds are for Trevor, for David and for Trevor.'

'You mean you have the baby Trev? Really!'

Trevor nodded.

David was excited, 'But how?'

Trevor adjusted his tie, 'I will explain all, but another time grasshopper. They are perfectly safe and sound in my breast pocket. We just have to keep our heads down until she, who will remain nameless, leaves in the morning.'

'Oh, Trev, next time you ply a dim-witted Frenchman with cheap wine to translate Le Telegramme, get one that can read. She will do the plaque thing tomorrow, Monday, not today. She will miss her baby, and we are surely going to prison, where French poofs and DJ's will abuse us.'

'David, my little unhealthy thinking friend, you don't even know if there are any French poofs or DJ's in prison over here. Most of them are locked safely behind bars in

England. Now, let’s get back to the Lac Dave, and don’t look or act like a diamond thief.’

‘Baby, Trevor, baby.’

OK, let’s get back to the Lac baby.’

They didn't see or hear Madame Rousseau at all that day. She must have slept through it, as did her entourage. They were careful not to drink too much and went to their rooms early before anyone spotted them for work or questioning. David sat on his bed reading 'Learn French In A Day'. Trevor spent hours studying his little gems. He looked like Gollum.

***

# Lerryn Cider

The far-reaching fingers of the trees
Trying to obscure the moon
Like cobwebs or frayed lace
Clinging to a white balloon

The shaky shimmering reflection
Of a lonely village light
On the calm, soft waters
A lost ghost in the night

I gaze the view in silent awe
The village green and fair inn
A warm spring twilight eve
Drinking the cider of Lerryn

Trefor Dylan Jones

2013

# Chapter 10

## Getting Banged Up and Losing the Baby

It was Monday morning, and the boys were helping in the bar. David was very nervous. He was cleaning bottles when Christian tapped him on the shoulder to wish him good morning. *Smash!* 'Good morning David. That was a fine bottle of Château Pichon Longueville Baron, and it's coming out of your wages.'

'I don't get any boyo, and anyway, you pay peanuts for posh wine over here.'

Christian retaliated, 'What would you know, you sheep shagging clown.'

It was cold, and the rain wouldn't let up. David noted that it had not stopped raining since he arrived in Brittany. Trevor had an answer for everything. 'It's worse in Wales, even the Queen reigns.'

It was soon to be 2014, and Trevor was looking forward to the new year and more surprises. He just remembered something he had read, 'Did you know Dave, that a Canadian man called Dick Cock will be a hundred years old next year? Now, grasshopper, imagine having a name like that.'

'Well Trev, there are plenty of Taffies called John Thomas.'

'Well done David. I see you are learning the art of comedy.'

Trevor was trying to think of some other weird facts for the new year. 'OK, not only is Beautiful Existence her real name, but this American woman has eaten and drunk nothing but Starbucks coffee and crackers since 1st January 2013 and will not return to regular food until 1st January 2014.'

'Why?'

'Dunno, you will have to ask Angie.'

It was nine fifteen and in walked Madame Rousseau looking smart and fresh and unaccompanied by her small army. Trevor saw her through the fitted mirror behind the bar. He kept his back to her. She approached him and said, 'Apportez-moi un jus d'orange.'

She walked away and sat in the lounge where she met two others. Trevor kept his back turned, cleaning glasses. Christian looked surprised. 'What's the delay? She wants an orange juice. Take her one.'

'Alright, keep your beret on. God, you're moody today.'

'Sorry Trevor, my mother has been very sick, and I was going to visit her last night on my bike as the car has a flat tyre, but some bastard has nicked my head-lamp, so I couldn't go. She died early this morning.'

Trevor blushed. *Oh well, in for a Euro.* He took the orange juice over to her and set it on the table. She was talking gibberish to someone and hardly noticed him. Not even a merci. Was this the same woman? He could see the chain and the outline of the purse beneath her blouse. He returned to the bar and cleaned some more glasses.

David pestered him for information, but there was nothing he could tell him. David was his usual nervous self. 'Let's pretend we're ill and get out of this place before her memory returns, and she checks her jewels.'

'Don't be silly David, just stay calm, she'll be going in a few minutes.' They had finished cleaning the glasses and were looking for something else to do, so they cleaned them again. 'This place will have the cleanest glasses in Huelgoat Dave. Let's clean the mirrors, at least it keeps our backs turned.'

Jean-Jacques had arrived with a thousand bonjours and shook hands with all and sundry. He was surprised to see the boys working so hard. He asked David for an extra-large coffee and sat at a table holding his head. He told the boys to take a break. David rushed upstairs without a word. Trevor joined Jean-Jacques and talked non-stop about quantum mechanics and string theory. Jean-Jacques thought he was talking about string driven Meccano sewing machines and admitted he had never seen one.

A large Citroen pulled up outside, and the chauffeur walked around and opened the rear passenger door. He stood like a statue, while she sat sipping her orange. She decided to stroll across the lounge to the front door. Jean-Jacques dashed over and opened it. Without a single thought of thanks, she stepped out to the car and waited for someone to open the rear door. The driver obliged and drove her to the forest to unveil the plaque. It was only a five-minute walk to the passage by the grotto, so David and Trevor decided to join the audience.

***

The square swarmed with people. The market usually takes place on Saturdays, but just this once the authorities changed it to a Monday. It was like Cardiff carnival day. There were more stalls than usual, selling everything from carrier bags to Breton flags. Food stalls, selling hot food from big black cauldrons. Cheese stalls selling every conceivable cheese available, and stalls selling various gourmet sausages. The square looks like a giant Wim's bar or a miniature Marrakech. People were walking on stilts, playing those daffodil shaped flute things. It was very noisy. Some wore traditional Breton costumes. The women wore big black skirts with coloured tapes stitched around the hem and small diamond-shaped glass beads sewn all over, glittering in the sun. They wore stupidly long white hats on their heads. Trevor said, 'If Marge Simpson had a hat, it would look like one of them.' The men wore baggy trousers and white waistcoats. Some were wearing big black, wide-brimmed hats. Everyone was shaking hands and kissing as usual. David and Trevor wove their way through the crowds. People had travelled miles to see the opening of the plaque.

They reached the unveiling area, situated at the forest entrance, where some of the larger boulders lay. It was busy, and hard to see or hear what was happening. An ornate oak panel, screwed to a decoratively carved wooden post was just visible under two red velvet curtains which Madame Martine Rousseau would pull apart sometime during the ceremony.

The Maire was giving a speech, but of course, the boys didn't understand a word of it. It sounded a bit Welsh, so he must have been delivering his speech in the Breton language. The speech lasted several minutes. Occasionally he would stop and smile, waiting for the audience to clap. Madame now moved forward. There was a multi-coloured string for her to pull. Each time the Marie stopped for a breath, she tried to pull the cord, but then he would start talking again. It was obvious that she didn’t speak Breton.

The overdressed audience was shivering. It looked like a Laurel and Hardy show. Now he stopped talking, and she was waiting. He said something in French, like, get on with it then, we don't have all day. A few people were laughing. She pulled the string, and to everyone's amazement, the curtains opened. It was a carved piece of Oak, with what looked like something written in Breton, French, and believe it or not English. Several dignitaries now progressed to the Maire's lunch. The crowd dispersed, and Trevor could now get closer to the plaque to read it. The top third had Breton writing. David thinks it's Welsh. Below this, a fancy squiggle and the middle section was in English, another squiggle and then French. Trevor read it aloud:

**Huelgoat Forest.**

**The forest covers an area of over 10 square kilometres. The enchanted forest of Huelgoat abounds with massive boulders and clear sparkling pools. The main path that starts here leads you to Le Chaos de Rochers or the Chaos of Rocks, and the Grotte Du Diable or Cave of the Devil. Here the water from the lake plunges ten metres below ground into a large cavern, the noise of the water is thundering. After the Cave of the Devil, the stream continues underground before re-emerging and winding**

**its way through the forest, developing into fairy pools with stepping stones and small bridges. All around are the beautiful water-smoothed boulders and rocks laid out in precarious positions. If you look hard enough, you will see the odd Korrigan (fairy) that inhabit the forest. Further into the forest is Le Camp d'Artus, an ancient hill fort and one of King Arthur's last resting places. Nearby is La Roche Tremblante, a massive boulder weighing over 100 tonnes, precariously balanced in such a way that a child can rock it.**

**This memorial honours the people of Huelgoat. Some of whom fought in the French resistance and lost their lives in the forest of Huelgoat fighting against German occupation.**

**Thank You.**

'We should have a gander about sometime in that forest Trev.'

'Yea.'

They moved away with their heads full of fairies and bigger stones than theirs.

David and Trevor settled for a coffee in the Tabac. Three wise men were sitting at the bar with caps on and wearing dirty clothes. The proprietor greeted David with, 'Bonjour, que voulez-vouse Anglais branleur.' All three men giggled under their breath.

David replied. 'Deux cafés au lait, s'il vous plait,' Trevor gestured with his hands. 'Big, big coffee. OK, big and white, with milk, lait.' He was fed up with David ordering big coffees in French, and then to see someone coming over with a couple of egg cups. They sat in their cosy corner to discuss the future. Black coffee arrived in three thimbles. That didn't bother David. He was rich. Well, soon to be. Trevor slapped his head. He always did this when he was angry. 'Is he taking the piss?'

They were here to plan how they will have their baby valued and sold. Trevor preferred the idea of travelling back to Wales to achieve this, but David thought this may be risky with customs and would prefer an alternative. They were in brainstorm mode, or combination of minds, as David liked to call it. David wanted to sell them in France. He had an idea. 'Patrick is a fence. I'm sure he could find a buyer for us.'

Trevor was still not convinced. 'Grasshopper, we hardly know him, and he would want a cut. What about a posh pawnbroker in Paris?'

David had another idea, 'What about eBay?'

'eBay, you twat. We're selling diamonds, not second-hand shoes-'

David stopped him. 'You are not supposed to say that word.'

'What word?'

'That word.'

'What, Shoes?' Trevor slapped his head. He tends to do this when he has thought of something stupid. 'I have an idea that might work. We could post them to a mate's house in Wales. Preferably, someone we don't like. John Davies would be an excellent choice. I've never liked him since he pushed me off my bike when I was four. We then get the ferry home and pick up the baby to sell in London.'

David was sceptical. ‘I wonder if they can scan the packet to see what it contains. Mind you, if they did that, it would be John Davies being shagged by a DJ.’

The door opened with a bang. The little bell above it fell to the floor. It was Patrick. He came bounding towards them. The proprietor greeted him in the same way as he did with David. The three men laughed. Patrick turned towards him and pulled him over the bar. ‘What the fuck did you say, matey.’ The two big men fell to the floor fighting. Trevor jumped up and tried to separate them. One of the men sitting at the bar also intervened. A woman, who had just arrived, ran out screaming. Before long the gendarme came and separated everyone. They took Trevor and Patrick out to question them in a police car. The police took statements, but Trevor didn't understand a word. Patrick spoke what sounded like fluent French, but with *fucking* being every other word. It happened that Patrick didn't normally speak French, so the proprietor must have thought he couldn't. The man, whose name is Yann, welcomed them with, 'hallo, what can I get you, English wanker.' That word *English* offended Patrick.

***

The police drove Trevor and Patrick to the local cop shop and put them into an old wet cell to calm down. Trevor was angry because he hadn't done anything wrong, well not so far today. What if they decided to search him? Oops! Oh dear. Was he here because of the missing diamonds? Stash the cash, but where? He might find somewhere in the cell, and then, if searched, he could retrieve them afterwards. There was nowhere suitable. It was just a tiny, empty stone room with a single metal bed and a thin plastic-coated mattress. There were a few loose stones on the walls.

While Patrick was busily earwigging at the door, Trevor was able to pry a stone out with the help of the trusty Swiss penknife he had bought from the corner shop next to The Buccaneer. He knew it would come in handy one day, He then wrapped the baby in a five Euro note and stuffed it deep into the hole, then replaced the stone the best he could.

He then sat patiently on the side of the bed, thinking about home, and the man who lives at number 71. Trevor had convinced himself that this man was a spy. He borrowed a pen from Patrick and wrote a short poem about the spy to try to keep his mind from thinking about prison. Patrick had one ear firmly against the door and repeatedly mumbled, 'What the fuck?

After, what seemed like hours, Patrick jumped back from the door. A gendarme entered the cell, accompanied by Didier (pronounced Did. E-A), another friend of David's, who lived in Landeleau, near Plouyé. He was small, scruffy, and overweight. He was wearing an old dirty oversized suit. 'Nous avons trié sur tout. We have sort everything out, and you now free to go. It was all malentendu, misunderstand. Gendarme thinks you part in the fight. Patrick is free also. Yann has been tolded off by police.'

Trevor asked Didier, 'Will they search me?'

Didier looked confused. 'Why they want search you? You are not criminal.'

Trevor was desperate to ask if he could stay, but that really would sound stupid, even for him. He could get Didier to tell them that he was doing a thesis on French police stations. Didier told him 'You not right in your heads, you ill or dément.'

Patrick was getting itchy feet and pushed Didier out of the main door. ‘No worries mate, let's get the fuck outta here. That Welshy is a few stubbies short of a fucking six-pack mate.’

***

They left and returned to the Lac, where David was waiting and looking fed up. The police had confiscated his car. He had seven days to make it legal. Everyone had a couple of beers. Trevor now got a chance to tell David where the gems were. He explained the situation, and they both agreed that to recover the baby one of them had to return to the police cell, and they both knew what that meant. Trevor said, ‘It's like getting banged up and losing the baby. What a miscarriage of justice!’

They decided to make Didier drive them to Carhaix (pronounced car-A) to get a burger. He complained, saying, ‘Chercher midi à quatorze heures.’ They didn't understand so just ignored him. Trevor sat in the back of the car. Carhaix was home to McDonald’s. The English would drive from all directions for miles, just for some proper food. Didier and David ordered a Big Mac and fries. Unfortunately, Trevor asked for chips and extra onions. It was a big mistake in France to ask for chips. They sat down, and Trevor enjoyed his Big Mac and bag of cheese and onion crisps.

***

# The Little Old Man at No.71

Flirting with the enemy
Cavorting with the foe
One man's lust for freedom
And who on earth will know

You take a dip, try your luck
Test the water, just a toe
It's murky, and it's deep
How could you sink so low?

Loyal to the hand that feeds you
Blow after blow after blow
Blind to the realities
Secure in the status quo

And now your treason reaches out
And will never let you go
The sun no longer shines
The winds no longer blow

Trefor Dylan Jones

2004

# Chapter 11

The First Noel, And the Turkey Trot

It was Tuesday, the twenty-fourth of December, Christmas Eve. The town had decorations and lights, although the bars didn't bother, apart from Angie's. Christmas was very different in this country. Every village had masses of adornments, but there were no Christmas trees.

French children put their tiny shoes in front of the fireplace, hoping Père Noël would fill them with small gifts like fruit, nuts, and small toys. In Wales they would hang up a bloody great stocking, hoping for Santa to fill with an iPad or iPhone. David's theory was, the bigger the stocking, the more stuff you will get. In some parts of France, Père Fouettard spanked naughty children. That was weird. In 1962, a law had been authorised decreeing that Santa would reply to all letters with a postcard. Any kid who wrote to Père Noël would get an answer, although its authenticity must have been in doubt.

Jean-Jacques had allowed David and Trevor to stay until the new year, on the condition that David worked behind the bar in the evenings. David loved working behind the bar even though he spoke hardly any French. All the posh guest's drunk wine or Champagne and the local riff-raff that had done the 'tour' of the pubs mostly spoke English. It all seemed to be back to front. The choice of wines was incredible but very organised, so if he didn't understand what they wanted, they could either point or get what he gave them. The average customer rarely knew the difference anyway. When he got a chance, David invented cocktails and fed them to Trevor.

'David my little guinea pig, try this. Mentally add the following numbers.

1000

20

1030

1000

1030

20

Now your total is 5000, right.

Wrong.

Now use Jean-Jacques' calculator, the total is 4100'

(If for some unknown reason you arrived at the correct answer. Believe me, you are too clever to be reading such a book as this. Go and find something suitable for a genius.)

The time had come to get serious and figure out how they would get Trevor arrested. They had a simple plan that couldn't go wrong, and it had a Christmas theme to it. Trevor was going to steal a turkey from the boucherie. Well, they called it a boucherie, but they sold more fish than meat. They should call it a fisherie. The French eat a lot of fish. In fact, apart from the horrible big bone with a bit of meat on it, seafood was the staple diet around here. Anyway, A gang of French Christmas revellers would catch him and hand him over to the police who would arrest him and charge him with *fowl play*. They would then take him to the cell in the police station where he would retrieve the diamonds. A simple reprimand or small fine for stealing the turkey and as Trevor liked to say, Bab's your aunty. It was a simple plot, effortlessly executed and bomb proof.

Trevor had done his homework. Marc, a student, who was working at the Lac in his gap year taught him all about the French and Christmas dinner. The French, being strange peoples, didn't just eat their Christmas dinner on Christmas day. Oh no, theirs is Christmas Eve as well, and they call it Réveillon, traditionally eaten after midnight mass, so Le Grand Lac Hotel would be open very late to serve Christmas Réveillon to their staying guests and other diners. This also meant the boucherie would also be open late, as the French tend not to buy their meat until the last minute. After Réveillon, it was customary to leave a candle burning in case the Virgin Mary dropped in for a drink.

They would eat another Christmas dinner on New Year's Eve, and then another on New Year's Day. The French enjoyed eating Christmas dinners. The French were gluttons so there would be turkeys galore.

Trevor had all day to prepare for his big turkey robbery. He called it his 'First Noel and the Turkey Trot'. They spent the morning downing coffee and planning the Penydarren bar repairs and, of course, discussing turkeys. After a spot of lunch, they relaxed in the bar. Trevor would visit the boucherie in the early evening when it was busy. In the meantime, they lazed around, drinking coffee. Trevor was writing a new poem but was too excited to finish it.

***

It was seven o'clock. Trevor was ready to do his work. He had a three-course meal in case he had to spend all night in the police cell. It was a better idea than the packed lunch that David suggested. It was raining as usual and was getting dark. He shook hands with David and joked, 'Mum, can I have a hamster for Christmas? No, you'll have turkey like everyone else.'

He strolled down towards the boucherie. The square was busy with shoppers. He was thinking, he should have cased the joint first, but then that might have been a little dramatic. The shop was bustling with customers, all trying to reach the counter. The French did not queue. He was looking for the turkeys. They were selling loads of beef, pheasant, lobster, pig trotters, and oysters. Lots and lots of oysters. It need not be a turkey. Why did David say turkey? Was it David that said turkey? So long as he got banged up again, he didn't care if it was a lobster. There were plenty of live lobsters there, in a fish tank, or a lobster tank. What is the difference between a fish tank and a lobster tank?

Trevor decided to grab a lobster and run for it. He was shaking with fear and excitement. He had never nicked a lobster before. In fact, he had never even held a lobster. They looked a bit dangerous. They had massive claws. Each claw was as big as its body. Nicking a lobster might be downright suicidal. Why should he be doing this? David should do the simple jobs. Trevor thought he was the smart one. If that was the case, why was *he* putting his hand into a giant fish tank? He should go back and tell David it was his turn or lie and say a pack of angry French turkey farmers chased him away.

He saw a live lobster once. It was walking over the shingles on Mumbles beach and was a lot smaller than these. It could have been a crab with long fingernails. Anyway, when you see pictures of lobsters, they have elastic bands around their claws.

The butcher disrupted Trevor's line of thought. 'On s'occupe de vous?'

Taken by surprise, Trevor said, 'Have you got any turkeys, la dinde, la dinde?'

The butcher was offish. 'Non, Je vais aider la personne suivante dans la file.' and served someone else.

It looked like it had to be the lobster. Would an oyster do the trick? *He might as well be hung for an oyster as for a turkey.* No, everyone would laugh if they saw him running off with an oyster. It must be a lobster. Fear of losing a couple of fingers was creeping in. Those claws were massive. Trevor thought, how wicked to keep all those lobsters in one tank. He should have left and called the RSPCA instead. He wondered how much damage those big claws could do. He had read somewhere that some lobsters were left-handed. He leant over the tank. His arm reached towards a giant lobster with claws like crocodile mouths. No, sod this. He walked out.

***

Trevor arrived back to an empty bar, apart from David and another man, who were sitting in the corner talking. David introduced him to Trevor as the Mairie of Plouyé, but before Trevor could reply, he rushed out, saying, 'Sorry, I'm late.'

All and sundry were coming in later to stuff their faces with, lobster! David had been inventing new cocktails and then drinking them. He looked at Trevor, expecting him to be carrying a turkey, and being pursued by the gendarme. 'OK, what went wrong this time?'

Trevor felt a bit stupid. 'Around here, Turkey is a country Dave, located in Western Asia. Why a turkey anyway? What's wrong with a penknife, or a small car? I was going to steal a lobster but bottled out. Have you seen the size of those lobsters?'

David sneered, 'You're a big pussy. What are we going to do now?'

Trevor had a simple solution. 'We will leave it until after Christmas when everything settles down a bit. Get me a large brandy, before Jean-Jacques arrives.'

David poured Trevor a brandy. David was feeling hungry as usual, especially after all that talk of turkeys and lobsters. They talked about the situation for a few hours. After several brandies, Trevor ditched the idea of joining the gendarmes or using explosives. He gasped and run out of the bar! Shouting, 'I won't be a minute, I've got an idea.' David entertained himself mixing cocktails. Floc de Gascogne, Pastis, Trouspinette, and a twist of lime. He called *it Gascoigne's Tears*. He was feeling a little unwell. Trevor eventually returned and said, 'I had a thought. It occurred to me that the diamonds may have gone right through the wall and fell on the floor outside, at the rear of the station.'

'Well did they?'

'No such luck. The walls are about a foot deep.'

The night went on, and staff, guests, and customers all started to arrive. Jean-Jacques and Christian sat down in the restaurant and played their guitars. Christian asked what the sheep shaggers could do to entertain. Trevor was quick to answer. 'David used to be a tap dancer until he fell in the sink.'

By the time it got to midnight, the place was buzzing, and then, almost as quickly as it filled, it emptied. Everyone went to midnight mass. Only Christian, Trevor, David, and a few staff remained. They talked about the six nations rugby match that will be starting on the first of February when Wales played Italy at two-thirty in the Millennium Stadium, and then England would take on the frogs in Paris. It was vital that he found a comfortable place to watch the rugby. Preferably one that sells beer. They would have to decide where to watch the games soon. Nothing was easy in this Country. Christian didn't understand rugby. He bored Trevor, talking about his paintings and prints.

At one o'clock, the crowds started to arrive, including priests, gendarme, and the Maire. Everybody wanted to sit at the Maire's table. He was like God here. Trevor was thinking that it might be worth kidnaping him and demanding a ransom.

The night went on, and on, and on. These people must sleep on very lumpy beds because getting them to lie on them is near impossible. David was eating a croque-Madame. Trevor commented, 'To the untrained eye, that's cheese on toast with a fried egg on top. Anyway, I'm on the diamond diet, and I've lost six stones already.'

They sat in a corner to discuss Homer Simpson. David and Trevor often talked about Homer Simpson late at night. They were always comparing him to people they met. Trevor had more info about Homer than anyone else in the world. Homer was Trevor's hero. The two of them often played quiz games. If Trevor ever got on that programme, Mastermind, Homer would be his specialist subject. David was always Magnus Magnusson.

'Who is bald, fat, stupid, crude, clumsy, lazy, a drunk, and ignorant?'

'D'oh! Me.'

'Correct.'

'What is Homer's father's name?'

'Abraham Simpson.'

'Correct.'

'What is Homer's favourite food?'

'D'oh! Nuts.'

'Correct.'

'What is Homer Simpson Syndrome?'

'The findings of a five-year study of more than 2,000 middle-aged people in France that found a link between weight and brain function.'

'Correct.

Merry Christmas Trev. It's Christmas Day, and we will soon be rich.'

'Merry Christmas Dave, Where's me prezzy?'

‘Where was mine when it was my birthday. You are a selfish little Welsh bastard? I will get you a Rolls Royce, but you will have to wait until we throw the baby out with the bath water. In the meantime, I will get you the hubcaps.’
Trevor gave David a definitive answer,

‘Go to bed you prat. We have to be up early in the morning.’

‘Goodnight Trev boy.’

‘Goodnight Dave boy.’

***

# *RR*

You stole my hubcaps, you bastard
You snatched them from my car
Yes, you took my hubcaps, you bastard
While I was drinking in Bob's bar

You drive a beaten-up Cortina
Not a Rolls Royce by far
But with shining bright new hubcaps
Inscribed with big bold letters, RR

You stole my hubcaps, you bastard
I've seen them on your car
Yes, you nicked my hubcaps, you bastard
While I drank with Bob and Laura

You say they came from Halfords
But there's no Halfords in France, liar
If you bought them from Halfords
You swam from Scaer to Par

You stole my hubcaps, you bastard
You forced them from my car
A Rolls without its hubcaps
Is like jam without a jar

Just because you're pathetic and poor
And I'm a superstar
Does not give you the right to do
What you have done to my car, bastard

Trefor Dylan Jones 2017

# Chapter 12

Seven Squabbling Swansea Seagulls.

It was Christmas morning, and the two Welshmen had hangovers. They both wanted to ring home, but Christian looked as if he was guarding the phone. He was more business-like than Jean-Jacques and checked the phone log regularly. Long distance calls had soared since David had moved onto the premises. Christian had already quizzed him about them. David said he would keep an eye on the staff. At least the log didn't list the destination of the calls. David had a mobile but rarely used it. It cost too much. Trevor had a brainstorm, 'Here's the plan grasshopper, I will occupy Christian while you make the call. I'll make mine later.'

'OK, Trev, cheers.'

Trevor walked to the main entrance and lit a cigarette. He pointed to the road and shouted to Christian. 'I never thought you would ever part with that picture of Joan of Arc.'

Christian ran to the entrance. 'I didn't. Someone's stolen it. Where did he go?'

Trevor pointed to the square.

Christian ran out shouting, 'voleur, voleur.' After a while, he returned, breathless.

Trevor was holding the picture. 'I got him. I went the other way and caught up with him by the tabac. I snatched the picture, but the little thief got away.'

'Thank you, Trevor. You are a hero and very brave and fit. You are not even out of breath. Let me buy you a drink.'

'Oh, thanks, Christian. I don't mind if I do. I've never seen such a huge bloke. You should screw your pictures to the wall. There are thieving bastards everywhere.' Christian was relieved.

'It's only a print, but it's been in my family for years, just as I told you yesterday.'

Wim rang the hotel to inform them that he had some news about Penydarren. Intrigued, the boys patiently awaited his arrival. They didn't wait long. Red-faced Wim arrived with Didier. They all sat at a table. David got the coffees. Wim started talking in his backward English. He had caught some squatters living in Penydarren. They have been kicked out by a few of his friends, but the windows and the old door will need replacing soon. Trevor asked Wim if they had done any damage.

'Damages already done is. The bar broken tis. The peoples cannot worse make it.' Trevor slapped his head. He always did this when anyone spoke back to front English.

Didier invited David and Trevor to his houses in Landeleau for Christmas dinner. Angie, Patrick, and a few farmers would be joining them. Trevor thought it would be fun. 'Why not, it will make a change from Huelgoat.'

David was busy on the phone. 'C'mon boyo, we're off to Diddy men's houses.' Everybody drank gallons of free coffee, and after collecting Angie, they left.

Didier drove an old English plated car, which made David nervous. He was still waiting to see what happened about his small accident.

Plouyé is on the way to Landeleau, so they inspected the bar as they passed through. There was a ton of letters and advertising pamphlets littering the floor. Angie was worried all that paper might start a fire!

They reached a small hamlet called Penker Lois, which was not as far as Landeleau. Didier lived there, although everybody said he lived in Landeleau. It's a bit like Dowlais and Merthyr.

***

They drove up to a small broken gate. There were two cars parked nearby. The white painted stone house stood in the centre of quite a large plot. A massive stack of logs leaned against an old outbuilding that had a broken window. The garden consisted of six-foot-high grasses, in the middle of which an old tyre was visible. There was a rotting conservatory on the front of the house with several broken windows and a sliding door. Another door led into the kitchen. Broken plates and old dirty mugs occupied the sink. At the far end stood a very dirty cooker standing next to a gas bottle. An opening to the left of the kitchen led to the living area where several bright red lamps were hanging from the smoke-stained ceiling's curved wooden beams.

Didier's house was typical of most French houses, dirty and scruffy. He did at least have a separate kitchen and an upstairs bathroom, which was most unusual. Because of this, his friends called him *Le Roi de Penker Lois*, (The King of

Penker Lois).
The large living room had a loaded wood burner, which emitted a lot of heat and smoke, and a big round table in the centre surrounded by a variety of old broken chairs. Patrick was sitting at it with a local farmer speaking French, (apart from every other word) and they were smoking a joint. Everybody shook hands, and the Welshmen introduced themselves to the farmer, Jules.

Didier disappeared for a while and returned with two large transparent plastic bags, full of what must be homegrown grass. Wads of money changed hands, and Angie took charge of the bags. 'I'll be the bellhop and stick these darlings in the trunk.'

Didier said he had better remove his magnets for a few hours and went to the corner of the room and opened a small cabinet on the wall. There was an electricity meter in it. He removed a magnet from either side of the meter and put them in a jar.

'I pay EDF pour deux heures every mois, and then they are no suspicious.'

Patrick looked up. 'He pays for electricity for a couple of hours a month. He's scared the fuckers will catch him.'

This interested Trevor. 'What are the magnets for then.'

'Those little fuckers stop the meter from registering any electricity. One each side stops the dial from spinning.'

David also took an interest. 'John, the electrician, rewires the meter.'

'That's OK if you send EDF regular estimated readings and keep a log of what numbers you have made up, but this little fucker's too lazy.'

He had prepared a meal of sorts, although there were no plates or cutlery. They started with bits of dry bread and pate.

Then came a large bowl of salad, on which he poured some oily liquid. A choice of cheeses and lumps of torn baguette followed. So, this was Christmas dinner. Cans of lager and bottles of wine littered the room. Bread was flying everywhere, and a mouse even dared to run across the room, and collect some from under Trevor's feet, for his own Christmas dinner.

They were all stoned or drunk or both and talking gibberish in different languages. Trevor was smiling. 'We sound like seven squabbling, Swansea seagulls.

Patrick found this very funny and couldn't stop laughing. 'What a fucking wallaby.'

Didier had an old boom box and selected a radio station that played British and American pop music. Angie tried to dance but kept falling over. The farmer was singing the wrong song, using the brush end of a broom that was full of cobwebs as his microphone. Didier tried to dance with Patrick, but Patrick was having none of it. He had a beer in one hand, a joint in the other, and was laughing like a hyena. Angie commented on Patrick's torn pants. Wim was singing, 'Tak me om county wose.'

The whole experience reminded Trevor of an old playhouse farce, where everyone came and went, and fell over one another. He couldn't stop giggling.

Pierre and another farmer from Plouyé arrived and bought some grass. Everybody fell over everybody else to shake hands. They all looked like English Morris Dancers doing the maypole dance without the maypole. The noise was deafening, and the room was full of smoke. Eventually, everyone fell to sleep, slumped on the table, or on the floor.

David woke up to use the loo, that was, the garden. Only Angie went upstairs. It had just turned five o'clock. David felt like he had been there forever. Trevor, still stoned, went outside for some fresh air. ‘David, there are no televisions in France. Haven't they been invented yet? Why is the sports bar called the sports bar if it doesn't have any sport? There's a telly in the bookmakers but all the programmes are about horses, and why doesn't Patrick buy a new pair of jeans?’

Once everybody was awake, they all sat down for a sobering coffee, before making their way, a mile or so, to Cleden-Poher, to visit Patrick's bar. Wim and Angie both closed for Christmas day, although Angie intended opening in the evening.

***

Cleden-Poher did not look like the most exciting village in Finistère. Apart from Patrick's bar, there was a corner shop and a bar/restaurant. Most of the houses were unoccupied (most looked like a bomb had hit them). Patrick had lived there since he emigrated from Australia seven years ago, and he was one of only a handful of residents left in the village.

He called his bar Le Poher House, and he lived on the premises with his wife! John, an Irishman who seldom came downstairs. They had plenty of parking space to the front of the bar for the many customers that frequented the place at weekends. The bar was double fronted, with shuttered windows, and had a covered patio area to the front, adorned with tables and chairs.

As they entered the bar, the first thing Trevor noticed was a giant television on one of the walls. It was the first one he had seen since leaving Roscoff. Oversized Marshall speakers and professional DJ lighting accessories were hanging from the ceiling. It looked like a typical Welsh nightclub. Patrick turned the bar lights on, but it made no difference. The windows had shutters closed over them and looked as if they had never seen the light of day. It was a spacious room, and everything was green. Even the floor tiles were green. Patrick supplied the drink and turned on the CD player. The traditional Irish folk songs drowned out Angie, who had been talking non-stop since she arrived. Patrick reminded everyone that the Four Nations Rugby would net him a fortune in February.

There was a closed sign on the outside wall, and yet the door opened and in walked two French couples. They had a quick conversation in French with Patrick and went and sat in a far corner.

Patrick had a chess trophy behind the bar. Trevor offered him a game.

'I don't have a fucking board mate. The nippers nicked the fucking thing. You any good then.'

Trevor smirked. 'Good, have you not heard of Trevorsky. I once played for Wales.'

Patrick looked a little bemused. 'Fair suck of the fucking sauce bottle mate. That's awesome.'

David piped up. 'Trevor, you never played chess for Wales, you are a lying little Welsh turd.'

Trevor had a quick response. 'I meant to say I played in Wales.'

Angie stopped talking and rolled a joint. After a few puffs, Didier started trying to speak English. Trevor told him that he spoke excellent English, and Didier agreed. 'I am taught by myselves. I rode book bout Anglais.' Everyone laughed, even the French couples in the corner. Trevor said Didier would make a great translator, translating French into gibberish. After a few lagers, Didier offered to take David,

Trevor, and Angie back to Huelgoat, which they accepted. It had been a long day.

***

The two men spent Boxing Day morning in the Lac, drinking coffee with Didier and Didier's friend Stefan, an artist and sculptor.

Trevor whispered in David's ear, 'He looks like one of those San Francisco type hippies we saw at The Hullabaloo Festival many years ago. You remember Dave? You wanted to be a Hara Krishna twathead.'

'Oh yea, Linda and what's her name? We thought we would never find the way out.'

'I wonder Dave, why these artists have to wear a smock covered with multi-coloured paint. If he could really paint, it would surely be on his canvas, not all down his front.

Didier was talking in half English about his ambitious plan to produce moonshine. He intended to make a still, that employed a car radiator, used as a condenser. Stefan was practical, and a part-time plumber. They will use Methanol, which the fuel store sold. As a bonus, they can sell Methanol locally as antifreeze.

Angie had given Didier a book called 'The Secrets of Building an Alcohol Producing Still', by Vincent Gingery. Didier asked David to *help him reads it as is foreigner language*. The factory would not take long to build as long as a few farmers helped. Didier and Stefan would start work on the still once all work on the factory had ceased.

Trevor turned to David, 'I almost forgot, you're singing here tonight.'

David looked puzzled. 'I can't sing. They only let me sing in the choir because my dad pulled a few strings.'

'Don't worry David, you don't have to work behind the bar, and Jean-Jacques is paying us.'

'Us!'

Trevor smiled. 'Yes, I'm your new agent.'

They ordered four croque-Madames. A croque-Madame was a croque-Monsieur with a fried egg slapped on top of it.

They spent the afternoon drinking and discussing all things from Patrick's weird sex life, to why motor-home disease is so prevalent in France. The boys didn't wander from the Lac all day. They were both wondering if Madame had discovered she had no diamonds, but neither mentioned it to the other. Nor do they discuss how they were going to get them back. Trevor decided. 'We will enjoy the rest of the holidays and worry about the diamonds later.

David was too tired to argue. 'OK.'

***

Now Didier might be stupid, but he wasn't daft. Any Breton, who owns a house in the country and can make a fortune supplying homegrown grass was not daft and could prove it.

He turned up at the Lac with Patrick, as his interpreter, and a business plan. He intended to build his underground moonshine factory soon and needed help. Trevor wished *he* could produce chloroform. David was impressed but was worried that creating an underground factory near the house may raise issues about subsidence. Trevor was more concerned about it blowing up! Patrick had a plan. 'We can dig out the underground booze factory a little way from the house. It will be a fucking great steel underground cage mate. He just needs four grand to make a start. He has two, I have one, and you, my lovers, have the other fucker. What do you think?'

'Let me sleep on it.'

'OK, now what the fuck do you think.'

David was contemplating. *Could he afford a grand?* 'How can you dig a big hole, erect a steel cage in it, and cover it for four grand?'

'The little fuckers a builder. The steel cage will be the biggest cost. All that fucking steel costs a fortune. The entry would be via a trap door, topped by imitation grass in the flat roof.'

Didier butted in. 'Mon grass, je vais fumer.'

Patrick told him to shut up. Trevor was warming to the idea and wanted to know how they would make the moonshine.

Patrick had all thc answers. 'Take a load of grain and allow the fuckers to sprout. Just as they are sprouting, kill the fuckers by drying them out on the flat roof of the factory. It's now malt. Mix the malt with hot water and keep stirring the fucking stuff. The sugar from the malt dissolves. Filter the solid stuff out and add your fucking yeast. Keep it warm. The yeast will turn the sugar into alcohol. Then you distil it through the radiator. Distilling it separates the fucking ethanol. Pure fucking ethanol boils at 78.4 degrees centigrade, and water boils at 100 centigrade, so heating it will make the ethanol separate. Then you sell the fucking stuff to all thcm French layabouts, and say, 'wrap your laughing gear round that mate.'

Trevor was impressed with Patrick's explanation, but he still had reservations and could imagine a giant explosion that killed them all. David thought Patrick must be a *fucking* genius.

David still had doubts. ‘A thousand quid is a lot of money Pat. What makes you think I’ve got a grand?’

‘A bit at a time. No fucking worries mate. I can always lend you some at my special Welsh boys interest rate.’

‘OK, we’re in.’

***

# Seven Squabbling Swansea Seagulls

Seven squabbling Swansea seagulls
Were squabbling the day away
They squabbled over everything
From chips to China clay

They squabbled every morning
And into the afternoons
They squabbled on the beach
And they squabbled on the dunes

One day one seagull asked
Why do we squabble all day?
The other six had no reply
And continued squabbling away

Trefor Dylan Jones 2014

# Chapter 13

## Le Médaille d'Honneur Pour Acte de Courage et de Dévouement

It was market day in Huelgoat, and it wasn't windy or raining. In fact, it was a beautiful sunny day, even if a bit on the chilly side. Trevor thought it was funny that David was trying to buy some cheese. ‘Avez-vous une Cheddar à vendre?’

The stall-holder was confused. ‘ce qui est Cheddar.’

David tried again, ‘Cheddar cheese. Avez-vous any Cheddar.’

‘Non.’

David ended up with a wheel of Brie de Meaux cheese and a bag of olives. That was close enough. Trevor asked David, ‘What happened after the explosion at the French cheese factory in Huelgoat?’

‘I don't know Trev. What did happen after the explosion at the French cheese factory in Huelgoat?’

Well, I will tell you, my little gravedigger. All that was left was de brie.’

David shook his head, and they walked on.

Next on the agenda was fish and chips in the Buccaneer. The pub was busy. David told Perran that they would come back later when he was not so full. Perran said, 'I am not full. I have only had a bag of crisps.' David was wondering why everyone was acting so stupid today. It could have been Angie's fault. She had been selling magic mushrooms that she grew in a secret garden in Huelgoat Forest. She gave Trevor a bag for some strange American reason, and he had been picking at them. David suspected, by the look of Perran that he had been eating them too.

It was just after twelve, and they decided to walk around town until Perran was less busy. Angie's place was rocking. She was selling slices of mushroom quiche to all who come into her bar. People were milling around looking like the walking dead. David grabbed a handful of mushrooms from Trevor, and they strolled around the lake. David shook hands with Claude Laffont, who was sitting outside his shed. He was frantically pointing to the middle of the lake. David thought he was trying to rent them a pedalo and kept saying, 'non.' He was still pointing and pulling at David's jacket. Trevor saw what had happened. There was a small girl who looked like she was in trouble. A crowd was starting to gather. Trevor jumped into the lake and swam to the girl. It was a big lake, and Trevor could hardly swim himself. He reached her and grabbed her. He held her head up and swam back. She was only about four years old. He laid her on her side and placed his ear next to her mouth and nose. Her chest was moving, and he could feel the air on his cheek. He checked her pulse. There was no pulse. Her mother ran over screaming. There was a big crowd of people, and it was getting bigger. Trevor hadn't much room. He was trying to remember how to perform CPR. He turned her gently onto her back and put the heel of his left hand onto the centre of her chest. The right hand on top of his left hand, and pushed down, making sure not to press too hard on her ribs. He remembered all this from a small leaflet his parents had given him when he was a kid. Thank god for his superior memory. Thirty compressions at 100 per minute. He let her chest rise between pushing down about two inches. She was still not breathing. He tilted her head back to open the airways and pinched her nose. It was the only thing he'd pinched today and wished he never had to. He took a breath and covered her mouth with his. Then breathed into her mouth for one second, twice. Her chest rose, and he repeated the procedure followed by thirty chest compressions. He continued this cycle of 30 compressions and 2 breaths. She started breathing and spewing water out of her mouth. She cried, and the place went wild with clapping and shouts of 'bravo, bravo.' The girl's mother hugged Trevor. He now felt a little embarrassed. Some of the men hoisted him onto their shoulders. Trevor was a hero.

An ambulance arrived and took the girl to the hospital as a precaution. There was pandemonium everywhere. A group of men carried Trevor into the square. All he could hear were shouts of 'bravo.' He thought he was in the Royal Albert Hall. David kept saying, ‘Put him down’. Trevor wondered what he meant. At long last, they lowered him to the ground, and David guided him into The Buccaneer.

***

Everyone in the pub greeted Trevor, including Perran and his wife with a standing ovation. Trevor imagined he was a famous conductor and bowed several times. It must have been the mushrooms. Perran had laid the best table with silver cutlery, and they were both treated to a massive plate of fish and chips. David said he was going to report Trevor to the police for child molesting. People were clapping and shouting 'bravo'. Trevor said, 'Is it the Last Night of the Proms.' After the fish and chips, there were ice cream sundaes. They looked even better than Giovanni's. Angie came in with a mushroom quiche for them to take home. Trevor thanked Angie. 'I would never have jumped in the lake if I hadn't been for your mushrooms. I thought I could swim. You could have killed me, you stupid cow.' They all drank a few Lerryn cider's and relaxed. It had been a long day. David went back to the lake to find his cheese.

It looked like trouble, Yann, the owner of the Tabac, came in with two gendarmes. They walked swiftly to Trevor's table. Yann grabbed Trevor. Trevor was trying to get loose. The big man had him in a bear hug that prevented Trevor from hitting him. To Trevor's surprise, the man started kissing his head. 'Stop that, you pervert.' Yann was crying. Trevor thought that this man had lost it. The policemen were laughing instead of arresting anyone. Angie shouted at Trevor. 'It is his daughter you saved. He is thanking you.'

'Oh.'

'The gendarmes are his brothers. They're very proud of you.'

Trevor glanced at them. 'Oh, it was nothing. It was all down to Angie. Go and squeeze her instead.'

David got back with his cheese and olives. He saw the commotion and ran back out. Angie had to chase him around the square before she could catch him to clarify everything. They returned to the Buccaneer. Yann and his police escort had left. The place was settling down, and there was more room to move. Perran had a phone call. The little girl had fully recovered. They all got drunk.

***

David had agreed to work behind the bar all day. Trevor was sitting in the lac drinking free coffee. He was disappointed that they didn't need to nick it. Jean-Jacques had told him he could help himself to free coffee forever. Everybody who came in greeted Trevor and shook hands. Even people passing by came in and shook hands. He got no peace. Angie came in with more quiche. Trevor looked at David, ‘This is getting ridiculous my little Welsh turtle.’ Angie spent a good half an hour talking to someone at the door before she eventually found her way to Trevor. ‘Hi Trev, I have some more quiche for you, and when you've had enough beer, I'll get the check.’

‘Thanks, Ang, how are you?’ He now wished he had not said that. Once she started talking, there was no stopping her.

Yann, from the tabac, walked in with a big cage covered with silk fabric. He dropped it on Trevor's table and removed the silk. It's an African grey parrot. He shook hands with Trevor and said, ‘C'est pour vous. Vous m'avez sauvé la vie des filles.’ He then left.

‘What did he say, Ang?’

‘He has given you a parrot for saving his daughter's life.’

‘What do I need a parrot for, I've got you, babe.’

‘They are very expensive Trev. If you don't want to keep it, he will not be offended if you sell it.’

The parrot looked at Trevor. Trevor looked at the parrot. ‘Can you talk?’ There was no answer. ‘It might be like David, can talk, but won't. How do I know if it's male or female, or how old it is?'

Jean-Jacques came over. He was not happy. 'You won't believe this. When one of the girls was dusting the chandelier, she found that the centre hanging glass globe has a cheap Christmas bauble in its place. It will cost several hundred Euro's to replace. If I ever catch the thieving bastard, I will kill him. Ah, an African grey. Very nice Trevor. It's not easy to tell the sex as they have no external organs. The feathers are lighter on girls. The males have flatter heads and larger beaks. The females are rounder. Also, the feathers near the vents are grey on the tips if it's a female. I think it's a girl Trevor.' Everyone clapped as if Trevor had just become a father. 'She is under six months of age as she has black eyes. I will give you five hundred Euro's for her.'

Trevor looked at the bird, then looked at the parrot. 'Jean-Jacques' friend Mathias, who once worked in the Congo National Park, said African greys can only talk gibberish. Therefore I will name her Angie.'

'Why, thank you, honey.'

'It's nothing. What do I feed it on?'

'How should I know, hun?'

'I wasn't asking you. Jean-Jacques, do you know?'

David shouted from behind the bar, 'Parrot food, prat.'

Christian shouted from his office. 'You could always feed her on Bullshit, sheep shagger.'

Jean-Jacques knew everything about African greys, 'A balanced diet of organically processed pellets and some nutritious fruit and veg. All obtained in bulk from the Super-U hypermarket in Pleyber-Christ. Thank you, please don't applaud.'

A thought had entered the Welsh man's head. ‘Where will I keep her?’

Jean-Jacques scratched his head. ‘She can live here until Penydarren is up and running. If you decide to sell her, please keep me in mind.’ Trevor wanted to keep her. He liked parrots and tried stroking her, but she bit him.

‘Ouch, Who's a pretty bitch then?’

Angie (the American one) answered. ‘Me.’

They spent the next two or three hours trying to teach Angie (the parrot) to talk. The other one could talk the hind legs off a muskrat.

***

It was New Year's Eve, and David had agreed to work behind the bar all day, again. Le Grand Lac Hotel was empty, apart from a Welsh layabout hero, who sat in the corner admiring himself and trying to write a poem about pirates and parrots. Angie was asleep on her perch. The parrot that is.

A small, smart gentleman entered the hotel, holding a briefcase in one hand and an umbrella in the other. He looked like Charlie Chaplin. He approached David and asked, ‘Vous êtes Anglais, Oui?’

David replied. ‘I'm sorry I do not understand. I’m Welsh you see.’

The little man looked down, holding his chin as Charlie Chaplin does, ‘Je recherche Trefor Dylan Johns.’

David understood, ‘Oh, Trevor Jones.’

The little man looked up, ‘Non, Trefor Johns.’

It was too early in the day for David to argue. The French dimwits always think their right, and yet they are invariably wrong. He pointed over to the corner. The little man walked over, waving his umbrella as Charlie Chaplin does. 'Escuse moi, Trefor Dylan Johns?'

Trevor looked up. 'Yes, nearly. What's your name? Charlie.'

David spat out a mouthful of some concoction he had developed. The little man sat down and fiddled with his briefcase. He pulled out a piece of paper and started to read:

'Trefor Dylan Johns, Vous avez reçu Le Médaille d'honneur pour acte de courage et de dévouement. Cette distinction est destinée à marquer des actes de courage et de dévouements.'

Trevor couldn't understand a word this little man was saying. He was talking so fast. He thought he must be some sort of policeman and had mistaken him for David the crook. The man continued with this rant. 'La Médaille d'honneur pour Acte de Courage et de Dévouement récompense, toute personne qui, au péril de sa vie, se porte au secours d'une ou plusieurs personnes en danger de mort. Elle peut être attribuée collectivement aux unités d'intervention et de secours avec, pour les personnels en service au moment des faits récompensés, le droit au port d'une-'

Trevor interrupted him. 'Stop, stop.'

The little man paused. 'Pourquoi?'

David jumped up and shouted for help. Christian was in his office studying the phone log. Trevor asked him to come over and stop this little man from talking non-stop. Christian came over, shook hands, and spoke to the man. They spoke for some time. Christian got up and yelled to David to get coffees and Champagne.

'Champagne?'

'Yes, sheepshagger, Champagne.' Christian sounded excited. He served the Champagne and turned to Trevor.

‘Trevor, you have been awarded the médaille d'honneur pour acte de courage et de dévouement. In short, it is a medal for bravery.’

This all bewildered poor Trevor, ‘What for?’

Christian was ecstatic, ‘What for! You twat, for saving the little girl's life. Her mother, who is divorced from the Tabac owner Yann, is an important employee at the Ministère de la Défense in Paris. She brings the child here monthly for the father's legal right to see her. She nominated you for the medal, and the Presidential committee authorised that you should receive it. It is a great honour.’

‘Is it the same one Bob Dylan got?’

‘No twat, you are not that important.’

Trevor was beside himself. ‘Terrific. Where's my Champagne?’

Christian laughed, ‘It's too good for a sheepshagger. You must go to Morlaix on the third of January to receive your medal. The little man said we could all go.’

‘You're not going anywhere unless I get a glass of Champagne.’

‘OK, don't spill it.’ They all looked around. They all heard someone say, 'Who's a pretty fucker then,' but there was nobody else in the room.

***

Wednesday, The first of January 2014. David looked at Trevor. ‘I have a new year's resolution.’ I will own a share of a distillery and sell moonshine in my pub.’ Trevor was scribbling something on a sheet of paper, he looked up,

‘How is that a new year's revolution? That is a pipe-dream my little grey parrot.’ He looked down again and continued writing.

‘What you are writing, Trev?’

‘A poem about Henry Morgan.’

David shook his head. ‘Is that the bloke who designed the Morgan sports car?’

‘Go away, David.’

It was Friday. Didier and Stefan had joined David and Trevor in Wim's. Didier said they were not planning on starting work until March, as the French need to get motivated. David told them that he would not be paying his share unless work began at once. Trevor was going to be the foreman. He insisted that all preparation work must be complete, and the steel must be on site, welded to form a cage before the middle of January. The meeting was short as Wim kept butting in.

***

The following day the boys were at Didier's house planning the work. They intended staying there for several days while the work was going on. Didier had borrowed a giant digger from one of the local farmers. Some of his friends would help them in the afternoon. Didier's eagerness impressed Trevor. The hole would be three metres deep and four metres square. Trevor insisted that it must be at least two metres from the house. They would then drop the cage into the hole, and the top boarded over with an aperture for the staircase. Patrick was out organising the steel and welding equipment. Didier's farmer friend Jules would be getting the electrics under-way once the cage was in place.

Patrick turned up in a flatbed lorry loaded with steel bars. They all unloaded the steel. It was heavy, and Trevor could not help unloading due to his back problem. David had only just become aware of this problem that Trevor had claimed to have had since birth. It took the rest of the day and all-day Sunday to dig the hole and get it square. Patrick and Stefan would be welding the cage the following morning, and indeed they did. They spent the rest of the day partying. The hired mini crane would arrive at midday on Tuesday to lower it into position.

It was Tuesday, and David woke up to a loud hooting noise. It was midday, and the mini crane had arrived. Patrick and Stefan had got the cage welded, and it was a simple matter of dropping it in the hole. Didier had just realised the factory was too small, and the amount of hooch made would only be enough to sell in David's bar. David had guessed that and had already named the liqueur *Grains* because it rhymed with Brains.

The next job was to line the cage with plywood and cover the top with floorboards. Trevor couldn't believe it all went so smoothly, apart from having to flatten the fence to get the crane in, and the one stupid farmer who fell into the hole. It was getting dark, so they left him in there all that night so they could retrieve him safely the next day with the crane. They all had an early night as there was plenty of work left to do tomorrow. Patrick, David, and Trevor all stayed the night.

‘Goodnight Dave boy.’

‘Goodnight Trev boy.’

‘Goodnight Pat boy.’

‘Shut the fuck up.’

‘Goodnight Didier boy.’

‘Shut up foreigner.’

***

After a late breakfast and a few joints, everyone relaxed and congratulated each other. David was surprised at how much they had achieved in just a few days. 'We should be operational well before March. We can then concentrate on Penydarren. The Maire of Plouyé has spoken to the Maire of Landeleau, and they have agreed to turn a blind eye to this and that for a small gratuity. By the time we're finished, our efforts will belong to half of Finistère.'

Didier made some more coffee, and they all sat quietly while David sang a song, *Just for Love*, by Quicksilver Messenger Service. Trevor went outside for a piss. He could hear yelling and rushed back in with his zip still undone. 'I think the gendarmes are here. Hide the dope and pretend you're normal.' David opened the window to disperse the smoke. Hc knew by now that if it were the police, they would smoke all their precious marijuana. They waited sometime before Trevor realised who was yelling. 'I do think we should get that farmer out of that hole before he screams the house down.

This did not amuse Didier. 'Oh dear, we better get him out of there.' They went out and rescued him. He was not happy and went home in a bad mood and never returned to help them again.

The boys returned to the Lac to honour their agreement for David to work while Trevor drunk free beer and talked to Angie (the parrot). They left Patrick in charge.

***

The sixth of January will stick in Trevor's memory for years to come. He might even write a poem about it. If he had learned to swim at school, or had he run a marathon, he would have won a medal, but he hadn't. He had certificates, some GCSE's, but no medals. He wasn't even brave. It had just been his lucky day.

They were all in the Lac preparing for the journey to Morlaix. Trevor had fed Angie (parrot,) and the whole gang gathered for the off. David recommended a count of heads. Trevor shouted out the names, 'Christian.'

'Oui, sheepshagger.'

'Angie.'

'Hi, yes, I was just going to ask...' Trevor ignored her and continued,

'David.'

'Yes.'

'Didier.'

'Excuser?'

'Patrick.'

'Good on ya.'

'Wim.'

'Ja.'

Each time he called a name, Trevor counted it on his fingers just as a child would.

'OK, we are missing someone, who's not here?'

David looked confused as he usually did. 'If someone isn't here Trev, how can they answer?'

'I'm not expecting *them* to answer, prat face. I was asking all of you if you know who's not here.'

Trevor had a recount. It was like a Welsh election. Someone was missing.

‘Whoever is missing will have to be left behind. It serves him right for being so daft and obviously French.’

Wim tried to speak, but Trevor told him to shut it. He tried again. ‘You listen not, but know I do, tis you.’

‘Keep quiet Wim, you half-baked Scandinavian.’

‘Trev,’ said David, ‘I think he is trying to tell you that you did not count yourself.’

‘OK, including me that's seven. Jean-Jacques, Stefan, Perran, and Jules couldn't make it. They all piled into the Citroen Berlingo that Jean-Jacques had kindly hired for them. They were off to the Place des Otages, Morlaix, where the building of Mairie de Morlaix stands. The excitement filled the air. Angie was talking non-stop to Wim, who couldn't understand French, let alone American. Patrick was arguing with Stefan about the Australian outback. The rest of them kept reasonably quiet.

When it calmed down, Christian gave a brief lesson about Morlaix. ‘The Saint-Mathieu quarter of the town is the oldest part of Morlaix, resting on the slopes of one of the three hills it is built on, situated south of the town hall where we will be going. Parts of the old town wall still exist. This area is wonderfully atmospheric & traditionally olde worlde French, with narrow cobbled streets with stone and timber-framed Tudor buildings where the second-floor overhangs. They have religious sculptures and gargoyles on their façades. There are plenty of bars and restaurants. The famous Maison dite de la duchesse Anne house which is now a museum is open to the public. This sixteenth-century house is one of the oldest in the town. Morlaix is home to France's tallest lighthouse, Phare de L'île Vierge. The railway station, served by TGV on the Paris-Brest line is next to the Viaduc de Morlaix, a feat of railway engineering built in 1861-3, and now a national historic monument. There is a square in front of the town hall called Place des Otages (Hostage Square) so named as it's here the Nazi's executed their hostages in December 1943. On Saturdays, the square is a busy marketplace. The town hall is a grand building. Agnès Le Drune, the Lord Mayor of Morlaix, will introduce herself to Trevor. She will then present the medal to him. The rest of us will be waiting in the foyer.' This reminded Trevor of the time David gave a lecture in Ross-on-Wye.

They were in Morlaix in no time and parked in the square very near the Bar ty Coz.

It was just a short walk to the magnificent town hall in the Place des Otages. Among the flags flying was a union jack. Trevor assumed that was for his benefit. It wasn't! They all piled into the massive lobby and signed a book. A tall man in a black uniform talked to Christian, and then lead Trevor into an adjoining room. The Maire was waiting for him and greeted him in English. Trevor wondered if he should bow or something. The door opened, and Didier entered. He told the Maire, he was l'interprète. She spoke a few sentences in French, then in English and finalised with, 'You have been very courageous, and I am pleased to award you this medal.' She handed Trevor a small wooden box.

Didier interpreted. 'Vous avez été très courageux, et je suis heureux de vous remettre cette médaille.

Trevor slapped his head. He tended to do this whenever he was embarrassed. 'You are translating English into French. How is that of any help to me you twat.'

The Marie giggled and shook hands with Trevor. They marched back out to the lobby. The gang were waiting and clapping. The whole procedure only took about ten minutes.

Trevor told them about Didier translating English into French. Wim said. 'He is gek. A stupid, very man.'

Patrick couldn't resist joining in. 'They are a pair of fucking wombats.'

David wanted to see the medal. 'Open the box Trev, let's have a look.' Trevor opened the small oblong box to find a gorgeous medal lying on a bed of silk. The round silver medal was attached to a blue, white, and red ribbon. David pinned it on Trevor's jacket. He looked like one of the old soldiers you see at the memorial in Dowlais in November. They all walked out to have a drink in Le Bar ty Coz. Trevor was still wearing his medal. The bar was small, dark, and cosy. They had a few drinks to celebrate and then made their way back to the Lac. It had been a grand day.

***

It was the evening of the sixth of January and David had only just realised that he never saw any Christmas trees during the festive season. How strange he thought. Trevor was in the noisy restaurant. He abolished all his theories about National dishes when he found out the famous dish around here was cheese on toast (croque-Monsieur). OK, it was better than the Welsh National dish because they put a slice of thin reconstituted ham on it.

Trevor had been learning about Galette des rois, another National dish. The Lac bar was empty because everyone was in the restaurant eating cake. Galette des rois was something to do with the 'Three Kings of the Epiphany feast'. It was to do with the old Misrule celebrations. It's baked with a small gift hidden inside it. Jean-Jacques had already told Trevor, it was a snowman in the Lac cake. The person who gets the gift in their slice of cake will be King or Queen of the party and gets to wear a gold paper crown.

Today was the Feast of Candlemas when everyone eats the galette. In Huelgoat there's fierce competition to be the patissier who makes the best galette des rois. Most of Trevor's friends were in Angie's bar as her cake always wins. Trevor was not getting involved. His parents made him wear a paper hat on Christmas day. How stupid. No one would allow Didier a slice of cake, as *Le Roi* was already his pet name.

Now Trevor could hear David singing to the parrot. Since David sang in the restaurant at Christmas, he had regularly been singing. To be fair, he sounded a damn site better than the local old men. He sang a Welsh version of a French favourite, Chanson du nouvel. It didn't matter what words he sang, they didn't understand. Sometimes the words were rude. The French also liked, Choral des Adieux (Auld Lang's Sine) so he gave them a rendition of that one as well.

***

They went to see Didier the following morning. The factory was coming on well. Stefan had fitted the stainless-steel flue liner and the staircase. He had also finished wiring the electric cables and fittings. The underground cable discretely connected to a fuse box in next door's cow-shed. Stefan was putting the still together with all necessary components, including the massive radiator Patrick happened to find nearby. There was still a lot of work to do. Patrick had run out of money. They needed about two thousand Euro's to finish the project. Patrick asked if he could sell Trevor's medal. He was only joking, wasn't he! The two Maires have stepped in to help, but they want a more significant share.

Ten percent each. At this rate, they won't make a penny. The boys had finished their stint at the Lac and will need to pay B&B if they wanted to stay any longer. They will tidy up Penydarren and live there. They had been too busy to think about the baby.

***

It had been the wettest January on record in Brittany. It was also very windy and cold. The Boys were clearing the debris from the bar. They wanted to prepare it ready to light the fire. The electricity was back on, and Patrick would be fitting the new front door and blocking up the windows later that day. He was busy that morning playing Boules for *Le Poher House Frogs*.

The logs were too wet to use. Didier was going to get some coal while securing the best deal for cheap Methanol to increase the strength of the moonshine. There was plenty of paper for the fire. Every time the postman passed, he threw a load of letters and advertising garbage through the doorway.

David had patched up the roof to the best of his ability, and Wim had supplied the couple with old beds he had promised them. He had shut his pub to go to Landeleau for a drink. The boys were going to join him, but they were weird peoples in Landeleau and didn't take kindly to strangers. The outside loo was now functional, and Jean-Jacques had supplied them with masses of old Telegrammes for its use.

They had transformed Penydarren into something like home. Once the fire was up and running, and they were warm, they would consider how to re-possess the diamonds. In the meantime, David had been finding out about the regulations for the bar. 'The Maire decided everything. It was like having the Prime Minister, Chief of Police, and the planning committee all rolled into one. If you wanted an extension on your house, you just bought the Maire a few jars, and Bab's your auntie.'

Trevor laughed. 'Yes, David.'

David had done most of the work. Trevor had done most of the talking. David poured a couple of coffees from his flask. 'Trevorsky, can you really play chess.'

'You will never know, grasshopper.'

***

# THE BUCCANEER

HENRY MORGAN TIS ME NAME
A WELSH BRED BUCCANEER
RAIDING SPANISH SETTLEMENTS
BY MY TROTH, IN THE CARIBBEAN
A NOTORIOUS AND SUCCESSFUL PRIVATEER
THE MOST RUTHLESS ALONG THE SPANISH MAIN.
I BE THE ELDEST SON OF ROBERT MORGAN, OF CAERAU
MORE USED TO THE PIKE THAN THE BOOK
I COMMETH TO JAMAICA AS A YOUNGER LAD
AND RAISED ME TO FAME AND FORTUNE BY MY VALOUR
I SAILED THE CARIBBEAN AND TAKETH THE WESTERN DESIGN
BY EVENTIDE MY FLEET TAKETH JAMAICA
WHICH GOD ALONE AND I SUCCESSFULLY INVADED AND OCCUPIED.

TREFOR DYLAN JONES 2014

# Chapter 14

The Sun Shines on Huelgoat, The Moon Shines on Penker Lois

.

Pierre turned up and invited the boys to join him for a demi at Angie's. They swiftly agreed and jumped in his car. Trevor always said, 'there is only so much work you can do in one day'. He often said it in the morning.

They arrived at Angie's, but it was difficult to get a drink as she was discussing a drug deal with two French estate agents. Just talking to estate agents annoyed the locals who regarded them as vermin. Pierre grabbed half a dozen Amstel bottles, and they sat down for a natter.

They discussed French women. David had been studying them. 'French women are practical Trev, and when they shop, they buy quality items that will last them for donkey's years. They didn't even eat croque-Madames. They all wore scarves and dyed their hair. French women were frank and forthcoming, even arrogant. They knew how to bring up children. French kids were polite to a fault. French women were generally slim and good-looking, unlike most Welsh women.' Pierre didn't understand, he thought they were talking about pig farming. 'L'intensification de l'elevage porcine en Europe au cours des dix dernieres annees a conduit a pratiques entrainant-' Angie abruptly interrupted him. She had taken a seat and had some interesting news for David and Trevor. 'I'm a bit hyped. I have spent a few bucks on a new high called sunshine. It's acid from the west coast. Anyone interested before it's all gone.'

'No thanks Ang, me and Dave will stick to the simple stuff until the factory and bar are up and running.'

'OK boys, I will have to find some other suckers, I better get back to work.'

Trevor carried on where he had left off.

'I think that's a bit strong Dave, I know loads of slim, good looking Welsh girls, unfortunately, they all live in England.'

'I'm going to find me a good French, Methodist girl to spend the rest of my life with, as I don't want to spend it with you.'

'Methodist? Dave, the only times you visited a church was when you went there to sing with the choir. You are no more a Methodist than I am.'

'You used to go to lots of them, OK, I know it was at night and only to rob the donation box. You have no morals.'

'I, my little Pinocchio bug, am an atheist. I hate religion, especially Catholics.'

There was a commotion. Two gendarmes pushed their way in to talk to Angie. Trevor thought they must be desperate for their dope, but a more pressing matter was afoot. Some coal was missing from the coal store, and a witness saw David in the store earlier, drunk. He had told the shop assistant that he was going to confiscate their coal as it was not Welsh. Angie pointed David out to the policemen who pulled him outside by his ear just as his mother did when he was a kid. They wanted to search Penydarren and take him off for questioning. He refused to go. David was having trouble understanding Angie's translation. She talked too fast. Trevor was telling David to go. ‘They will put you in the cell, where you can retrieve the baby.’

David said, ‘it's the principal. I'm innocent. I did not go to the coal store this morning.’

Trevor was telling everyone his friend was guilty.

‘I'm innocent.’

‘No, he is not, he is guilty.’ No one could understand why Trevor was stitching up his best friend. ‘I saw him take the coal.’

‘No, you didn't.’ The gendarme couldn't understand them. They couldn't understand the gendarme. Pierre was asking Trevor why he wants his friend in prison?

‘I will tell you later. David, don't be daft. When did you ever have morals? Now is not the time.’

‘But I didn't do it.’

‘David, shut up. Take him to the cop shop, the thieving little Welsh bastard.’

‘But Trev, If I go to prison I will miss the six nations. Patrick said we could watch every match at Le Poher House.’ In limped a very intoxicated Didier.

‘I got coal for David's houses. Not Wels coal. French.’

That clarified the situation. Didier took the coal and was shouting to Lorent, the coal store owner, who was out the back. Lorent heard someone shouting and joking that Welsh coal was better than French coal. Didier had phoned earlier, and Lorent told him to take a bag of coal and pay him later, as he would be busy counting the Methane. No one went to prison. Trevor was fuming, but still managed a new quote, ‘The wise man does not walk on hot coals but puts them on the fire.’

***

The hooch factory was complete. The flat roof was going on. The gendarmes were making house to house enquiries about twelve steel girders that vanished from a neighbouring farm.

The right equipment was essential when making moonshine. Contamination excluded the use of radiators for making the condenser due to the materials used in manufacturing. Stefan was using one because it was free. He had an electric pot to make the mash, which filtered into a pressure cooker. (The electricity to run them came from the neighbouring farm, yes, the same farm where all that steel disappeared from). From the pressure cooker, copper tubes ran to the radiator. (The copper tubing came from the blind man's plumbing shop. He couldn't identify the thief on account that he couldn't see). The radiator stood in a large glass lobster tank (stolen from the Boucherie), filled with running water from next door's stream. A flexible pipe connected the lobster tank's drain hole to a large plastic bucket via a cheesecloth filter.

Didier was using cheap methanol to increase the strength of the liquor. Methanol vaporises at a lower temperature than ethanol. Alcohol concentrations above about 50% alcohol by volume (100 proof) are flammable and dangerous to handle, especially true during the distilling process when vaporised alcohol may accumulate in the air to hazardous concentrations, so Stephan installed a chimney for adequate ventilation. It should prevent the underground hooch distillery from blowing up.

Patrick had gone to Morlaix to buy ingredients for the moonshine (cornmeal, sugar, and yeast). David thought this was a bit premature, but Patrick gave him a headache, so he let him get on with it. They spent the last few days finishing the project. Considering none of them were builders, it didn't look bad. They didn’t meet many problems. A slight incline on the flat roof was essential so Didier refitted it to allow for this. The moon will shine in the middle of March.

Didier was taking all and sundry out to lunch. He had difficulty finding everybody. When things got complicated, he always shouted, ‘Chercher midi à quatorze heures.’ It was a favourite French expression and meant something like, *people are making things more complicated than they need be*. The literal translation was *to look for noon at two pm*, and that made less sense. It was more like you were trying to do something too late or to do something impossible since noon was before two pm, but that was just like the idiomatic French. Trevor said, ‘I’m on the garlic diet, and I’ve lost three friends already.’

They all climbed in the back of an old flatbed Renault for a 'midi' at Le Meurice, on the road to Huelgoat. It took no time to get there. It was a large room in a converted house with four huge tables that each sat about thirty people. The place was busy and very smoky and noisy. They were lucky to find any room. It was a cheap and cheerful place that was nothing like its famous counterpart in Paris. You wouldn't want to see the kitchen. The café offered a 'plat du jour' (set menu of the day) which included a small salad starter, main dish (little meat on the big bone), with couscous and a basket of baguette, a dessert, a cup of coffee and as much wine as you could drink. The salad was at a self-service bar, with a choice of rabbit food that included chopped carrot, tomato slices, beetroot, boiled eggs, olives, lettuce, beans, sweetcorn, tuna, and small boiled potatoes. For dessert, you could choose between a yoghurt, cornetto, tarte de pomme (apple pie) or creme brulée. Price was just ten euros. They all eat, and as in French style, it took two hours to enjoy a small meal and lots of wine. If this were Wales, a police car would be sitting on the opposite side of the road waiting for customers to breathalyse, and indeed, they would have a very productive afternoon. David asked Trevor if he would prefer lobster to the main dish. Trevor laughed and told him not to be so shellfish.

***

The moonshine factory was busy in January, with Patrick and Didier trying alternative methods to make the alcohol stronger and cheaper. This little chimney that stood alone on a hill in the middle of god knows where was bellowing out poisonous gasses at a rate of knots. Trevor always kept himself at a prudent distance, at least a mile away.

They had managed to develop a drink of sorts. It would blow your head off, but would be profitable, and was useful for lighting bonfires. David tried a small glass and was ill for two days, but he was a weakling. Didier must have alcohol poisoning by now, but he was still drinking the stuff all day.

The Welsh boys were sitting on two orange boxes discussing the six nations.

'Trev, I know we must retrieve the baby, but what about the six nations. Wales are playing Italy tomorrow, and the

English are playing France. We must watch it. Patrick is putting on all the games. I haven't seen a telly in years.'

'Trevor retorted, 'Yes, you have, you have seen Patrick's.'

'Yes Trev, but it wasn't turned on.'

Trevor was in deep thought. 'Have you been to Landeleau David.'

'No Trev.'

Trevor had an idea. 'Landeleau is a lovely place. The pub has a telly. The pub's called Chez Christian, and they do not like the English. They are fervently Breton.

'But we are Welsh Trev.'

'Grasshopper, they do not know that. We go there to see the England-France match, then cause a riot. Let's face it, England will thrash them. Landeleau doesn't have a police station. They will take us to Huelgoat where we will retrieve our baby, and by this time next year Rodney we'll be millionaires. Only twats and sheep would get that one, so you should. Let's face it, I blew the turkey trot, and you blew the coal thing. Now we can both make amends.' David looked confused, as usual. 'Amends. That sounds a bit religious. Will we get beat up?'

'Maybe, for thousands of Euro's.'

'How can I support the English Trev, have you forgotten the fourth of August 2007.'

'I realise sunshine, that the fourth of August 2007 will stick in our memories like an apricot turnover, but this is important. For once we will have to act stupid. Can you do that, David.'

'I can try Trev.'

'Then David, my little Welsh leek, we will march forward, and we will be English for a day... Half a day. Have you got any English clothes?'

‘English clothes? I thought we all dressed the same Trev! I haven’t got corduroy trousers or a Mackintosh. Will they notice?’

‘I'm joking David.’

‘Jolly good Trevor. One cannot wait to participate in this awfully grand acting game. It may well be balderdash, but it will be a most delightful and pompous bit of fun.’

‘Quite right David, just a little piffle to get us locked up. What. Pass me a napkin, would you, dear chap.’

David started singing. ‘Please direct me to my abode, I am fatigued, and I wish to retire. I partook of a small beverage approximately an hour ago, and it migrated directly to my cerebellum.’

***

# Solemn Sunday

Red frocked men clutching candles of faith
They search the stave for notes to weave
Wrapping themselves in holy chords
Hot candle wax stuck to their sleeve

While the faithless pomp lovers survey the time
It takes to worship idols of stone
Praying, 'give me more bread, or it's Satan instead
Am I a Christian or am I a clone?'

The leader pours water from jug to jug
Straining his eye under tarnished felt
There are no glowing objects in the pulpit of course
He must be afraid he might melt

Fantasy drives the hypocrite and fool
Into thinking, he's one step ahead
But when the dawn breaks, and he finally awakes
He will find himself still in his bed

Trefor Dylan Jones

1995

(First published 1996. The International Library of Poetry)

# Chapter 15

The Six Nations Clash.
(Wales, Brittany, America, Australia, The Netherlands, and Cornwall).

A new month and another chance to retrieve the baby. Trevor was sitting on the pavement cleaning his shoes. He was looking forward to 'winding up' the Landeleau residents. ‘I might write a poem about them. I will call it 'Laughing at the Landeleau Louts'. It should be fun.’

David was a tad more cautious. ‘I should write it before we leave Trev, you might not get the chance otherwise. I notice you always clean your shoes when you're nervous. Who else ever cleans their shoes?’

‘I’m not nervous. What have I got to be nervous about my spring chicken?’

The door opened and in walked Didier. He had a red face and was shivering. He looked like he had aged a few years since yesterday. ‘The boisson alcoolisée is good. Why you paint shoes Trevoir? I rest now.’ He fell into a chair and was unconscious within minutes.

David looked concerned, ‘He samples that hooch too much Trev. He will kill himself if he is not careful.’

‘Don't worry my little Welsh rabbit, Didier is a man of steel. We better get walking. I'm not letting him drive us.’

The boys walked to Landeleau. It's about three miles. None of their friends, apart from Didier, would take them, as they want to keep their heads! David thought that the two stone heads outside the Mayor's office could have been the last two Welsh boys who came to these parts. He shivered. The road was quiet. David and Trevor were talking about what they were going to do once they were rich. ‘Trev, you're not really going to the Bahamas or wherever, are you.’

‘No David. I am staying here with you and all your strange little friends. I will be drinking Pastis in your bar and writing poetry on your walls.’

David smiled. ‘Funny the houses are without attics, isn’t it? And all these shutters on the windows. Must be dark. Can you play boules Trev?’

‘David, you sound like a half-wit, shut up.’

David missed Dowlais. ‘Do you miss Dowlais, Trev. I miss all the snails. Whenever we went to your gran's, we had to carefully avoid the snails on the steps. I miss the snails.’

‘Are you delirious David. Don't tell the locals about the snails. They will all move to Wales. They love snails.’

‘That's nice Trev. I didn't realise they were so loving towards little animals.’

David started to sing. ‘I remember the face of my father, as we walked back home from the mine. He'd laugh, and he'd say, that's one more day, and it's good to see the sun shine. I remember my mother was smiling, as I set out to make my own way. She seemed to know that I had to go, but I'd come back home one day.’

Trevor joined in for the chorus. ‘Take me home to my family, take me home to my friends, take me home to where my heart lies (out of key) and let me, let me, let me sing again.’ It was the first time Trevor had sung with David. He felt quite emotional.

‘Fancy a jog Trev.’

‘No.’

‘Come on. I'll race you to the crossroads. It's only a few yards.’

They ran to the crossroads. Trevor was out of breath. ‘Do you remember the poem about running the London marathon I wrote. I know it sounds soft, cos I can't run, but I always loved watching the marathon. All those people clapping and all.’

‘Trev. I don't understand your poems, but they sound clever. It's February. I must phone home soon. my mum will be worrying.’

‘You sound like ET. Phone home.’

David checked the time. The Wales-Italy game would be over soon.

They reached the village of Landeleau. There was a pub sign in the distance. It must be Chez Christian's.

***

They walked into Chez Christian's. It was a long building. There were magazines and papers on the left, followed by four or five tables and chairs. There was a serving hatch to the right with the usual display of cigarettes and a long bar, crowded with stools and men dressed like Welsh miners. At the far end was a large television. They had been watching Wales-Italy.

Christian was a small man, with a broad smile. Trevor commented, ‘Another Christian, Oh my god.’

‘Very funny Trev.’

He was talking to one of the men at the bar. Trevor shouted, ‘ENGLAND.’ followed by three loud claps.

‘Trev, can't we drink a beer before you get us stringed-up?’ Trevor squeezed between two burly farmers, pushing them apart.

‘I bet you haven't got any Brains, in fact, you look like a demented frog, and don't call me a wanker in French as I know the word.’

‘Pardon, que prenez-vous.’

‘Just get me two beers and hurry up.’

Someone shouts, ‘Deux bières, Christian.’

He passed them two lagers. The Wales-Italy game has ended. Wales won, and Trevor had to stop David cheering. ‘David, don't forget, this lot hate the grease-balls as well.’ They sat at a table, pushing one man aside. ‘Be careful Trev, we don’t want to be locked up before the England-France game begins.’ After a few drinks, the game started. Trevor was yelling, ‘ENGLAND, ENGLAND.’ France scores a try after just thirty seconds. The place erupted. Everyone was pointing at the Welshmen and laughing. After about a quarter of the game, the score was England 3, France 16. The bar was in hysterics. The boys were feeling a bit stupid. This joyous crowd were not going to fight anyone. In fact, someone had bought them a beer each. France leads at halftime. England 8, France 16. The smoke in this place was making it difficult to see. Most French-men smoked. The boys did, but usually something a bit stronger. It was back on, and another plan was about to backfire when England started playing magnificently. 11-16, and they were catching up. England went ahead. 18-16. Trevor was shouting all sorts of obscenities. He had been acting this part so well that he thought he was English. It got better for England. 21-16, With only a few minutes to play, England were winning 24-19. The English had won, just as Trevor had predicted. The Welsh did know a thing or two about Rugby. David was laughing at everyone. Trevor stuck his fingers up, and the locals were out of patience. There was a riot. Bottles and glasses everywhere. Tables overturned. It looked like a John Wayne film. Christian was shouting 'Nous avons gagné, nous avons gagné, nous avons gagné.'

That must translate to, 'gang up on them,' thought Trevor.

The gendarmes arrived. Trevor asked, 'Are you going to frog-march us out of here?'

'Oui.'

They were frog-marched to a van and shoved in the back. David had a black eye. Trevor was hiding under a table when this happened. The gendarmes were excited and spoke gibberish to one another. Oh dear, Trevor thought he heard, *Nous avons gagné* again. Don't say the police are going to gang up on them as well? Hang on. They were driving in the wrong direction. Huelgoat was not this way! Châteauneuf-du-Faou was this way. Trevor banged on the wire separator. 'We are going the wrong way.'

The policeman answered in English. 'Oh, I am so sorry. What direction is the gendarmerie where we will lock you up until you start respecting our Country? Now keep quiet, or there will be more charges brought against you.'

The other cop, who was driving, looked over to his friend and shouted. 'Nous avons gagné.'

Trevor was worried again and asked. 'Just what does that mean?'

The reply was comforting in more ways than one. ‘We won. I was talking about the Rugby. We scored a try and converted it in the last minute.’

***

They arrived at the police station in Châteauneuf-du-Faou and were banged-up. David was nursing his black eye. ‘All this, just to end up in the wrong town. How do you do it, Trevor?’

‘Don't blame me. How did I know that we were coming here? I've never even heard of the place.’

‘It was all your idea. Anyway, I’ve been told it is a pretty seaside town.’

‘Oh, that’s nice to know Dave. They are going to lock us up for who knows how long and all you can tell me is that it is a pretty seaside town. I’ll remember to tell my mum that if they allow me to write her a letter.’

The police treated them well and gave them coffee. After just twenty minutes in the cell, one of the cops, who spoke English, told them they were free to go. They didn't even have to stay overnight. Another policeman, who also spoke a little English said to Trevor, ‘We rang Huelgoat to confirm who you are. You have the médaille d'honneur pour acte de courage et de dévouement.’ He shook hands with them both. David thought they could get away with anything now. Under normal circumstances that would be a good thing. The policeman did offer them a ride to Huelgoat as that seemed to be where they wanted to go. They refused the lift.

They had a nice walk in Châteauneuf-du-Faou. It was bigger than Huelgoat.

‘I thought you said it was a seaside town, Dave. I see no sea if you see what I mean.’

David had a good look around. He climbed on a wall. ‘There is no sea to be seen. I think I can see a pub. Did you know the inhabitants are called Châteauneuviens?’

‘I don't care. Where's the pub.’

They walked a short distance past a big new post office.

‘I wonder why they have a new post office Trev.’

‘I don't know, perhaps the old one burnt down. Perhaps the postmaster was a Welsh prat.’

They walked through a large car park and reached a pub. There was music. As they entered the small building, they saw a jazz band at the far end. It was busy. They heard English people talking about the jazz festival that took place every year. David was getting very good at saying *deux bières*. They each had a beer. The English couple were leaving to go to another pub as this one closed early. Our intrepid Welshmen followed.

They walked around the corner and alongside a canal. It was not long before they reached another pub beside the canal. It was a large, glass-fronted building. As they entered, Trevor enquired as to how they were going to get home. ‘It’s late, and I don’t fancy sleeping with swans.’

‘I have my mobile. Didier or Patrick will pick us up.’

‘Ring Didier, I'm not in the mood for fucking this and fucking that.’

David was about to ring when he remembered. ‘Didier's probably been drinking that poison all day. I'm not sure I want to travel with him. I could ring the Maire of Plouyé, but I don’t want to disturb him at this hour.’

‘I didn’t think you knew him that well Dave.’

‘Oh, no I don’t.’

‘What about a taxi?’

‘We only have enough money for a taxi or a few more drinks.’ They had a few more drinks.

David liked this location, Sitting in a bar with big windows and panoramic views of the canal. There were swans and narrow-boats. A footpath followed the canal. ‘When I’m wealthy Trev, I will have a bar like this.’

They considered walking along the canal as the map on the wall made it look like the canal went in the direction of Plouyé. Trevor was too tired. He had an idea. ‘Right Dave, I want you to start talking to me about the medal of honour and raise your voice.’

‘You are such a big head Trev. I'm not talking to you about your undeserved medal.’

‘David, my little buttercup, when this lot hears about it, they will buy us lots of beer.’

‘Trevor,’ David shouted, ‘where do you keep your médaille d'honneur pour acte de courage et de dévouement. I thought you were so brave saving that little girl from certain death.’

The bar went quiet, just a few whispers. Someone approached David. ‘You are the Englishman, who saved the life of the girl in Huelgoat, yes.’

‘Yes, that is I.’

‘No, it's not, it's me. He is a lying little Welsh toad, and I'm Welsh, not English.’

And that was it. The drinks kept coming and the hours passed. A nice old lady gave them a lift back to Plouyé. Clever Trevor!

***

# The Running Man

Here comes the running man
Chasing shadows on a hot April day
His journey begins with expectations
But they have dissolved by half-way

Recalling wet winter mornings
Trudging along the darkened trail
Cold face, wet feet, numb hands
Past the range, the halt, the jail

Now the sun causes his grief
There's no hiding from the heat
He feels the burning on his neck
And the blisters on his feet

The well-wisher's chant and cry
'Keep going. You're nearly there.'
The running man faces the wall
His path blackened and bare

He passes the markers, one by one
Wishing the next was the last
He thirsts for water and glory
'Am I running too slow or too fast?'

He runs into the final mile
The smiling spectator's cheer
'Is it for me these smiles are cast?'
No more thought of pain or fear

Here comes the running man
Fingers numb and Knees that sting
He feels brave and all-conquering
Saying, 'I accomplished this great thing!'

Trefor Dylan Jones

2012

# Chapter 16

The Stars Shine Like Diamonds, But They're Not.

Penydarren was looking more like home. It had a door, of sorts, and the window holes now had shutters to keep the rain and cold out. The EDF man had connected the electricity, but only one light-bulb worked. Most of the wiring was dangerous and needed replacing. There was a log fire burning, and it felt good. It was still raining. Finistère endured the wettest January since records began, and a red alert was in force as forecasters warned of huge waves and extensive flooding.

Didier had been to Wim's to get a baguette and a large piece of cheese to share. He sat in a corner soaking wet, eating, and reading a paper. Le Monde was the favourite national paper around here. The Welshmen sat by the fire eating, and quietly discussing Leonard Cohen songs. Didier looked up. 'Madame Martine Rousseau had arrested been pour fraude.'

Trevor took an interest. 'Do you mean fraud. Read it to us.'

'Madame Martine Rousseau a été arrêté pour fraude, en ce qui concerne le vol de ses diamants célèbres.'

'No, in English you twat.'

'OK, I try. Madame Martine Rousseau has arrested pour fraude. She claimed or said her diamants had been thieven and wanted 120,000 Euros from assurance. The assurance company, er, how you say, did not believe, and policemen came. The diamants was in the safe place, metal box with cle, key. But they not there. She goes flee.'

Trevor looked at David. David looked at Didier. Didier looked at a scruffy cat with a big bald patch, who was then sitting by the fire.

Trevor looked down at the cat. 'Glass, they must be glass.'

David asked, 'Why are you talking to a cat?'

Trevor looked up at David. 'You see boyo. She would not travel the world with real diamonds around her neck. That would be stupid. They were in her safe. When we stole the fake ones, she tried to con the insurance company.'

'I see what you mean Trev, she combined the theft with fraud. It looks like we will be going to Paris. C'mon Didier, let's go and have a drink with Wim.'

Trevor turned to Didier, 'I wonder where she would flee to.'

'She no flees anywhere, she goes flee. She is flee, sorry, I mean she is loose. She not prisoned but flee to go. Assurances must pay.' Trevor winked at David for some strange reason. Was he on the turn?

Trevor wanted to go to Huelgoat first, as they needed to pick up the parrot. Patrick had been hanging around the Lac trying to teach the parrot to swear. Didier drove them all to Huelgoat, and they retrieved the parrot, even though Jean-

Jacques had offered one thousand two hundred Euros for her and the gilded cage. David suggested that they owned up to the chandelier ball and replaced it using the parrot money.

‘You're a soft little prick David, and the bird is not for sale, it was a well-deserved present. Now shut up. I've remembered who produced *I'm Your Man*.’

‘I’m Your Man, The Leonard Cohen song, Who?’

‘That's for me to know and you to find out my little dense friend.’

They had another cup of coffee in the Lac and finished a half-smoked joint. Trevor convinced David and Didier that they were hungry, so they went to The Shit and Shovel to share a large pizza. They took the parrot with them. As the waitress approached the table, Angie (parrot) started whistling 'take me home’ and continued with some speech that sounded very much like 'Who's a pretty fucker then.' The waitress looked shocked. Trevor knew who taught her that. ‘It's OK Dave. She's French. She can't possibly understand that, can she?’ The four of them shared the pizza and returned to Plouyé. David spent the whole journey complaining about sharing a pizza with a parrot. ‘Four cheese and Pepperoni Pizza is not parrot food.’

***

The three of them were desperate to get to Wim's. Why? Because there were only two stools in 'The Sports Bar'. When they got there, Patrick and a stranger had already taken them. Didier made his way to the sun lamp. He was wet through and shivering badly.

‘You got the fucking DTs Didier. You oughta stop drinking that hooch. It'll be the death of you.’

'Shut you up, kangaroo imbécile.'

'Don't call me a kangaroo you little fucking turd.' David had to stop them as usual. 'I was just coming to see you two fuckers. What the fuck's the John Dory.'

David put Angie's cage on the bar and ordered some beers. Trevor leaned against the wall and told Patrick what had happened. 'This stupid Welshman and myself have been conned. That bitch, Madame Roussie or whatever her name is, ripped us off.'

Patrick looked surprised. 'What the rich Sheila from Paris? What a fucking downer. Why would she want to rip off you fuckers? You've got fuck all.'

'It's a long story, Pat.' They all had a drink.

'Who's a pretty fucker then.' They all looked at Angie, then they all looked at Patrick.

'Why the fuck are you all looking at me? Why the fuck don't you buy some more fucking chairs Wim?'

'Why you did no buys new fuckin twousers?'

'Learn the fucking lingo. You half pissed Pygmy Possum.'

David was sitting on a box looking gloomy, thinking about all the time he and Trevor had wasted digging for fool's gold or Dumbo's diamonds. OK, they hadn't exactly been digging but still. Everything they did went wrong, but for some reason or the other, they usually came out of it smelling of roses. He asked Wim if he could make a quick local call. He rang his mum to assure her that everything was going well, and he would be coming home next month for a few days. He just wanted to cheer her up, but she sounded disappointed. She must have wanted to see him sooner. He asked how his dad was. She said he looked ten tears younger and was always smiling.

They chatted away for ages while the other's planned a day out somewhere. Trevor wanted a day at the seaside. Patrick liked Morlaix. Wim thought they should go further. To Paris or Holland. Didier suggested Spain for cheap cigarettes and sell grass over the border in Morocco.

'Morocco, that's where we get the fucking stuff from, You red-faced fucking hyena.' No one wanted to go to Carhaix. David hung the phone up and suggested they go to Africa to see Angie's relatives.

'More like Didier's fucking relatives.'

That caused a few giggles. They agreed on one thing. They were going to Huelgoat again today.

A police car pulled up outside, and in walked two gendarmes. A tall skinny one and a fat one. Patrick gasped, 'What the fuck now?'

Trevor made a comment about Laurel and Hardy, but it didn't look like a laughing matter.

The tall skinny gendarme yelled. 'Je cherche Daffydd Llewellyn.' Everyone pointed at David. 'Je vous arrête pour conduire une voiture Anglaise avec aucun impôt ou l'assurance.'

Patrick translated. 'Your fucked Dave, the wooden-tops want you in the slammer. Expect life without parole.'

The tall skinny gendarme then handcuffed David, and they drove him to Huelgoat. It confused him as to why not Châteauneuf-du-Faou, but at least he would get there before the others.

***

They reached the police station, and David went in, accompanied by the overweight gendarme. It was a small, old building. The inside was very basic. Just a desk and a couple of doors. The skinny cop took the handcuffs off, and the other one showed David a paper he must sign. After signing and dating, he took him to the cell to wait. The door to the cell remained open. He thought he was only in the cell because there were so few chairs in the office. David kept muttering, 'Would you believe it.' He remembered that bloke on telly saying it in that series, *something in the grave*. David was now in the same little cell that he and Trevor had been months trying to occupy. He sat on the edge of the metal bed and awaited his fate. Didier, his 'personal translator' had turned up. He looked ill. He told David, in his broken English that he had ignored a letter, sent to him in Penydarren advising he must attend the police station. No doubt that ended up in the fireplace. He would have to attend court for not responding to the letter about his car. They will prosecute him for not having English car tax or insurance, and for driving with four bald tyres. Didier was going to try to help the situation by aiding the police.

David sat quietly, looking around the room. He was looking to see if he could find the loose stone in the wall. It would at least use up some time. It reminded him of another telly programme he used to watch, *The Crystal Maze*. The five Euro note wrapped around the fake diamonds would be worth recovering. That would buy a couple of demis. A demi is about half a pint. French men are afraid to drink any more than that. He walked around the room, and it didn't take long before he found the loose stone. He wandered over to check it out, and with a gentle wiggle and a pull, was able to remove it. The fakes were still there, wrapped in the five Euro note, just as Trevor had said. He shoved it in his pocket and sat back down.

About half an hour passed before Didier returned. He said they could make a lasting deal and all charges dropped if David agreed to the following. When Penydarren was up and running, he must make it a comfortable police bar, with free beer and cigarettes. They also wanted a photograph taken with Trevor, wearing his médaille d'honneur pour acte de courage et de dévouement. Is this the world's most corrupt country? David had no choice. It was blackmail. How could two dishonest Welshmen keep up with this crowd! Wales 0. France 1.

The dodgy deal accepted, and they left to meet the gang at the Lac. They drove back laughing about Didier's negotiating abilities. Didier said, 'I deserves a médaille d'honneur.'

***

As they walked into the Lac, they heard a shout. 'The other fucking sheep shaggers here.'

David grinned, 'Very humorous Patrick.'

Everyone was there, sitting around a table, weighed down by empty bottles of lager and full ashtrays. David was interested to know why they didn't take him to Châteauneuf-du-Faou. Angie (the New York one) described in detail, 'Plouyé is under the authority of Huelgoat, while Landeleau, just a few miles up the highway is under the authority of Châteauneuf-du-Faou.' David nursed his eye.

'I wish I knew that before I got a black eye.' Didier got up to go to the tabac for cigarettes. David asked if he could get him a pack of Marlboro. He pulled out his five Euro note, and the stones rolled onto the table. With bottles everywhere, the table now resembled a pinball machine. Angie picked one up. 'What's this.'

David looked at Trevor. 'I don't suppose it matters now anyway. I found your loose stone.'

Trevor smiled, 'That's alright glass shopper, the diamonds are all yours. You will be rich.'

Angie asked David to pass it to the expert, Patrick.

'It's alright Ang, their only glass. Even an Aussie could tell the difference.' He handed one of the glass diamonds to Patrick, who already had his loupe to the ready. Patrick inspected the jewel. 'This little fucker ain't glass.'

Trevor paid attention. 'It can't be real. It wouldn't make any sense.'

'Well it's no fucking diamond, it's zirconite or possibly moissanite. Yep, this fucker's moissanite.'

David looked at Trevor. 'Zirconite, moissanite, glass. It's all the same. Worthless-'

Patrick butted in. 'Obviously, if these fuckers were high grade, two fucking carats, round brilliant fucking diamonds with no visible inclusions, you fuckers would be looking at anything up to five hundred Euros a piece. You got how many of these fuckers?'

'six.'

'I can give you two hundred.'

David stood up and done a funny little dance. 'Two hundred Euros. Trev, that's better than a leek up your arse'.

'Yes Dave, we can have a few dozen beers with that my little toe-twister.'

'No Trev, *I* can have a few dozen beers with that. You said I could have them.

'Ah, now David, my bestist buddy, I was a tad hasty there. Can we re-negotiate the situation over a few drinks?'

‘I suppose I would be willing to discuss it, Trevor. And what percentage is your starting offer?

‘Get the drinks in Dave, and I’ll have a think about it.’

‘I'm only joking Trev, and it’s your round.’

David collected the diamonds from the table and the floor and handed them to Patrick.

‘Hang on,’ Trevor intervened. ‘How do we know he isn't going to run off with them?’

‘I'm a responsible fucking fence you sheep shagging Welsh pig, as honest as the day is fucking long, and where will I run off to, fucking Hatton Garden, prick?’

Trevor smiled, ‘OK, faceted points taken.’

Everybody had another drink, and Didier, who hadn't grasped the conversation, left to get the cigarettes. Patrick offered the boys a cheque. ‘No thanks Patrick, we can wait.’

‘Come to my bar tomorrow afternoon. I should have your one grand two hundred by then.’

‘You mean just two hundred Patrick.’.

‘No, One thousand two hundred. That is two hundred a piece. Oh no, I've been fucked by two Welsh Moby Dicks, I could have got away with two hundred for the six. Shit, am I a fucking stupid Irish Aussie or what?’

There was a resounding ‘Yes.’

The two Welshmen got very drunk. That would be just enough to refit Penydarren with some stuff from the *Ti-Recoup* and stock up. Trevor would stay on for a few more weeks, but then he would get back to the valleys. Well, that’s what he thought!

***

**Dear Leonard**

I sit here at my desk trying to find a way
To tell you my hero, how much I care
But I cannot find the words to say
And just sit here empty, without a prayer

If I wait here long enough, maybe a thought
Will find a way to escape this dire reality
Writing to an image of a ghost I bought
Only one of us is real, and that is me

You could reveal all those poems and songs
To a world of lovers and sinners
And you could express the rights and wrongs
To both the losers and the winners

From Suzanne and Marianne to Joan of Arc
Your eternal lovers you have laid bare
And have shared for all to hate or love
And for all your worshippers to share

I sit here at my desk trying to find a way
But time moves on as my pen lays bare
I have now pondered here most of the day
And still, I have no words to share

Trefor Dylan Jones 2017

# Chapter 17

Penydarren And the Hoarse Maire.

It was a bright Sunday morning, and it was not raining. Didier had taken the boys washing over to Angie's. She had been kind enough to do their washing since they left the Lac. She washed and ironed everything, then gave the clean clothes back to them in separate parcels. David often found Angie's sexy underwear in with his. She always apologised and said it was a mistake. David didn't believe her. They would have to buy a small shed to house a washing machine, as there was not enough room in the bar, and they couldn't get one upstairs.

Didier returned in the early afternoon to take David and Trevor to Le Poher House. Patrick was sitting at a table watching Everton overcoming Swansea to reach the FA Cup quarter-finals. ‘Come on you ripsnorters, wipe them Welsh arses with those black swan snot rags.’

David shook his head, ‘Do you have to be so crude?’

Patrick greeted them with, 'Sorry, I didn't see ya. Arvo lads. What the fuck's on?' They sat at the table and exchanged pleasantries. Patrick delved into his pocket and produced a wad of notes. 'There you fucking go.' He handed Trevor the notes. David wondered why he hadn't given the money to him. Trevor counted the cash, and to his astonishment, it was all there.

They agreed to ask Patrick to help them. Didier and Stefan had already offered to help. They gave Patrick the job of organising the tradesmen as he was bi-lingual. Patrick was ecstatic, 'So, I will be a middleman, a fucking site foreman. That's me game lads, a fucking fence. Yeah, why the fuck not. What the fuck.'

David made it clear that *he* was the boss, not Trevor or Patrick. 'I want a simple Welsh themed bar, not the super casino Trevor has in mind, nor the surfing cocktail bar complete with barbecue that you have in mind. We will start at the top and work downwards.'

'Fair dinkum Dave, you will be up and running in no fucking time, and if you run out of money, no worries. I can lend you some at a more than fair interest rate. My last transaction netted me a fuck load of dosh.'

David looked at Trevor. 'Last transaction. Wasn't that us?'

They ironed out a few details and sunk a few more lagers. The new bar furniture would be simple and elegant. Patrick had already coerced some oak timber from the Maire of Landeleau and Stefan had agreed to design and build the bar etc. Didier would supply the cheap labour. They would start as soon as possible. The most urgent jobs first. The roof repairs followed by making the place secure with a new door and window frames. David and Trevor returned to Penydarren for a good night's sleep.

***

David whispered, ‘Trev, Trev. I think we have burglars downstairs.’

‘Burglars? David, my little ray of sunshine, we have nothing to burgle. It is probably Angie learning French.’ They got up and crept downstairs. Trevor sent David first.

‘Morning possums. The gang is here to mend your fucking pub, but first, breaky.’ Patrick handed the boy's bacon sandwiches. The first they had seen since they left Wales. They were still warm.

‘Fantastic. But where can you get bacon sandwiches in France?’

‘Oh, the fucking misses makes em. He's a terrific fucking cook.’

Angie squawked. ‘Who's a pretty fucker then.’ She was looking at Patrick.

Three of the local farmers, including Jules, who they had met before, were outside sitting on the back of a truck. They were eating croissants and drinking mugs of coffee. It was before eight in the morning. David thought he must be dreaming. They started work soon after breakfast and were hard working. A car turned up just after nine with Didier and Stefan. Trevor had wildly underestimated the commitment of this bunch.

Before long, work was underway. The gang were retiling the roof and repairing the ceiling. The upstairs was being re-boarded.

Come lunchtime, David invited everyone to The Sports Bar. Apart from Didier, the French declined the offer. They went to have a midi.

'We won't see them fuckers again today.'

David doesn't care. They all worked hard. Patrick was right. The bar would be up and running in no time. As they were entering, Wim greeted them with a big red smile on his face. It was redder than usual. 'Patrick, look wot I gets for customs.'

Patrick laughed. 'They don't need any more fucking tanning lamps.'

The bar area was clear of boxes and six new steel stools now adorned it.

'Fuck me, you Dingo, that's great.' They all sat down for a drink. Three tanning lamps kept everyone warm.

David went into some detail about what he wanted doing tomorrow, after some time, Trevor interrupted, 'OK David, that's enough for now. We should spend the rest of the day Thinking and planning. Sorry, I meant to say drinking and tanning.'

***

The next day was warmer than usual. It was now mid-February. The gang turned up at Penydarren with Angie. Patrick's 'wife' had made bacon sandwiches for them again. The boys thought they were in heaven. Patrick got his bacon from an English pig farmer in Cleden-Poher that Yann had introduced him to after their bust-up. The shops didn't sell rashers of bacon in Brittany despite there being more pig farmers than flies. David decided that this would be his regular bar food.

Most bars, even tiny ones, had a microwave and sold croque-Monsieurs. David would sell bacon sandwiches made with thick rashers of bacon, Breton bread, and English mustard. French mustard tasted like warm tea. Ah, Yes, he would be the only place that sold tea. David had learned the delicate ability of gently submerging a tea bag into boiling water to no ill effect. Catering type coffee machines were expensive, and he knew the French wouldn't drink Nescafe. They don't use milk so tea without milk would be a cheap alternative. He might even try different flavours.

Angie looked stoned. ‘David darling, are you good? If you buy some new pants and suspenders, I'll treat you to a night at the movies.’

David thought she had been going through his washing to thoroughly. Patrick shook his head. ‘Pants and suspenders? You mean jeans and bracers, you stupid bitch. Your English is fucked. Didier speaks better Pom than you.’

David looked at Angie, ‘Have you been on the mushrooms again?’

‘I had some on a couple of pancakes with maple syrup for breakfast.’

‘Yuck’.

Angie smiled. ‘The Vampire Academy movie is showing in Carhaix this evening. It's in French, but there are subtitles in English. I promise not to talk all the way through it.’

‘Not tonight Ang, I've got too much on. Maybe later in the week. Anyway, if it's got subtitles, I don't care if you talk all the way through it.’

A concrete lorry was due at around eleven, so everyone had been preparing for this with a big clean-up operation, and shuttering placement. Didier was the chief organiser of this. Patrick had organised two new double-glazed windows and a new door. The windows cost a fortune, but Patrick said they would be unique as Stefan was having them embossed or something. 'Ask Stefan. The fuckers will arrive next week.'

They stood outside as David explained the next level of operations. Everyone was enjoying this, and the cost so far had not led to borrowing from Patrick at his special Welsh interest rates. 'The large windows either side of the front door will be embossed with something apparently. There will be a sign above the door that reads, PENYDARREN in red and green. Inside, the red and green bar will be situated to the left rear, with two tables and chairs to the front of it. On the right, there will be a stage. The space in front of the stage will be for head-bangers and dancers. All this would fit in this tiny space nicely.'

The concrete lorry had arrived, and all hands were on deck to spread it before it dried. As a thank you, David arranged a day out to Le Poher House on Friday to watch the Wales-France game. His kindness had no bounds.

The game starts at 8 pm, so Trevor thought one thirty was a good starting point. That gives them six and a half hours to drink, smoke, and eat. Patrick will pick up the boys and Wim. Didier will get Angie, her friend, and Stefan. The others will make their own way. David raises his hand 'Who's going anyway?'

Trevor joked, 'I thought you David, of all people, would have known. Leigh Halfpenny and the rest of the squad.'

'Funny, ha, ha.'

'OK Dave, my little toe curler, there will be you and me, Didier, Angie and her friend, Stefan, Wim, Patrick, and Perran, the Cornish-ish-man from the Buccaneer. Oh, and Jules.'

***

It's Friday morning, and David got a call on his mobile. David never got calls on his mobile. It must be a double-glazing company. He answered it. It was Patrick. He had a brilliant idea. His friend, Christophe, had a minibus. He could borrow it, and they could go to the English pub in Carnoet that sold real ale and had a big telly. It would be a fun day out. David agreed. They would all meet at Le Poher House as planned and Patrick would be waiting with the minibus. It took Trevor ages to tart himself up. They had a croque-Monsieur at Wim's and returned to Penydarren to wait for Patrick.

Patrick turned up at about one and drove them to Le Poher House. Everyone met up, and the handshaking thing began. Angie introduced her friend Adele, a petit French girl with mauve hair. French women all coloured their hair. David counted everyone, and to his amazement, they were all there. They jumped on the bus, and off they went to Carnoet.

Carnoet was a small town the other side of Carhaix. It was less than an hour away. David and Angie were singing Leonard Cohen songs to cheer everyone up!

The pub, Les Fous (The Fools), was not in the town, but nearby on the main road. The pub sign had a picture of a joker on it. Patrick introduced Ben and Elizabeth, the English couple that owned the pub. After all the handshaking, they took them on a tour of the grounds. They had a large outbuilding (microbrasserie), where they brewed their ale. The pub was a nice size and looked British. It had soft seats and a proper bar with three real ales. Orson ale has a dog on the label, Duc de Carnoet has a duck on the label, and Old Stoat has, (you've guessed it) a stoat on the label. Ben and Liz were talking endlessly about their beer, but no-one was interested. Orson Ale, named after their dog, was in turn named after Orson Wells, was a delicious golden beer, and the Welsh boys were in their element. The French and Wim opted for a lager, although Stefan did try a small taste of Old Stoat.

There was a television in one corner, and they all gathered around it, even though the game didn't start for hours. Angie was flirting with David. 'Vampire Academy ends today, and you will have to take me to Paris to see it. We can stay the weekend.' David was a bit concerned that Angie had such an obsession with vampires.

Some heavy drinking got underway. David only had a few Euro's and wanted to combine the money, but he was the only one. Ben brought a large plateful of sausage rolls to the table. It was like being home. Angie was talking non-stop to her friend who didn't understand much English, let alone American. The television was on for the pre-match talk, but it was in French, so Wim, who only spoke a little French and even less English was translating for David. It was hilarious. This pub was so British, anybody who wanted to smoke had to do so outside. How primitive. The game was on, and Wales took an early lead. They ended up hammering the French, 27-6.

Didier had to pay Trevor twenty Euros. They all drank more beer and left for home. It had been a good day.

***

Progress was good. The gang had now been working for a couple of weeks, and they were almost ready for opening. Just a few finishing touches left. The place looked fantastic.

As you approached the pub, you could see a big red and green sign that reads PENYDARREN, and a bright flashing Brains Bitter sign Trevor had secretly sent over from the Tredegar Arms in Dowlais. It was not flashing because of smart technology. It was flashing because it was faulty. The windows Stefan organised were superb. The left one had a dragon etched into it. The right one, a Breton flag. The red door between them had a small green dragon painted on it.

On entering, the bar was on the left and made of a dull steel framework that resembled a full-sized dragon, with a polished wooden bar surface laying across its back. Fancy lights hung from the ceiling to light the bar area. To the right was a raised carpeted stage area. A spotlight marked the spot. The outside loo now had twin seats. Lovers could go to the toilet together. How romantic was that? Didier hadn't convinced them that they didn't need a urinal. Jean-Jacques had presented David with a picture of a traditional Breton woman who resembled Marge Simpson, which he hung behind the bar. The Maire had gifted them with a light-up canvas picture of a snow-street scene. It had little led lights in it that brought it alive. Trevor was intrigued as David insisted he hardly knew the Maire. Wim gave them a tanning lamp! David decided against a telly. On his day off, he could always go to Le Poher House to watch telly. Nobody knew who gave them the new red and green carpet. David loved it as he had the only bar that didn't have a tiled floor. That's all that mattered to him. Perran insisted he had left a box of twenty-four pasties, but David only found an empty box and some crumbs.

The extra tables and chairs were arriving on Wednesday from the Ti Recoup. Didier will be collecting most of the stock from the *Giant* in Morlaix and the official opening day would be on Saturday week. The local musicians would be playing their daffodils and singing trad folk all day.

David and Trevor were discussing Trevor's birthday, which he celebrated on the thirty first of March, due to him being born on the first of April when in walked Angie with a short, stout man. He was wearing a pullover with a black trilby and a long scarf. Angie smiled, ‘Hi folks, this place looks real good. I love the racoon thing holding up the bar. May I introduce to you, Claude, the Maire of Plouyé. He does not speak Welsh but would like to talk to Trev. He cannot speak to Trevor, as he only speaks French. Yes, he definitely does not speak English. I speak a little French, and I speak English, which is the same as Welsh, so perhaps-’

Trevor had to intervene, or they would have been there all day. He couldn't help saying, ‘Angie only stops talking when her mouth was full.’ That was subtle for Trevor, but David knew what he meant. ‘What does he want anyway?’

Angie went on, ‘The council needs an English speaker to stand for conseiller municipal in Plouyé.’ She looked at Trevor, ‘You will not be elected. The residents think you're weird. You just put your name forward, and that will be the end of the matter.

‘Ang, I might be a bit thick, but if I am not going to be elected, what is the point of putting my name forward?’

‘The population of Plouyé has a high percentage of foreigners. He cannot find an English speaker who has the time or the brains. When he asked Patrick, I bet you can't image what Patrick said?’ Trevor thought he could answer this one to within a fuck or two,

‘Oh yes I can,’ he said.

Angie laughed, ‘He said... Merci, Non, and there were no swear words.’

Trevor butted in again. 'Sorry Ang, I would love to be a conseiller, but I will be going home soon.'

Angie turned to the Maire. 'Il est désolé, mais il va très bientôt au Pays de Galles.' They had a short conversation, and the Maire seemed to be trying to shut Angie up. Trevor said there was only one way to do that. The Maire spoke slowly and sounded like he had a cold. Everyone shook hands and then Angie turned her attention once again to Trevor. 'What about until you leave?'

'Don't be soft Ang. I can't speak French. How would I be able to help?'

The Maire turned to Trevor. 'I can help, but I don't want the foreigners to know I can speak English, or they will come to me with all their complaints. You will not be elected like Angie said, the locals think you're weird.' He took a dirty handkerchief from his trousers pocket and blew his nose.

'I am not weird. I would make a great councillor, ask David.'

The Maire intervened. 'It would be a pity if I had to close this bar down before it even opened. Fire regulations, moonshine, opening hours, smoking.'

Trevor looked at David. 'The crafty little monkey. I suppose if there is no chance of being elected.'

The Maire happened to have all the necessary paperwork in his pocket. Polling day will be next Sunday.

***

# Who's A Pretty Fucker Then?

Alluring, winsome, angelic, appealing,
Beauteous, bewitching, stunning, charming.
Comely, cute, dazzling,
Delightful, divine, enticing.
Exquisite, arresting, fair,
Gorgeous, graceful, lovely.
Magnificent, pleasing, pretty,
Pulchritudinous, glamorous, radiant, ravishing.
Resplendent, shapely, splendid,
Good-looking, engaging.
Statuesque, stunning,
Sublime, attractive.

Trefor Dylan Jones

2014

# Chapter 18

Daoulas.

Tuesday, March the fourth. This morning was only the second sunny, wet-less one since he arrived in France. David was outside brushing his teeth. He turned to Trevor, who was sitting on the pavement. ‘Patrick is picking me up at ten, we are going to Le Poher House to borrow some glasses.’

Trevor was preparing himself for a day's drinking. ‘I'm coming too, aren't I. Anyway, we are getting stacks of new glasses from Coreff.’

‘No, you better wait here in case something turns up. We just need a few extra wine glasses. I won't be long.’ A car pulled up. A smiling face looked out of the open window.

‘What the fucks happening me beauts.’ David quickly jumped into the car, and it sped off into the sunset.’

‘Will this be a bog standard meet or are we all getting fucked up.’

‘I will tell you when we get in the bar.’

When they got to Le Poher House, the whole gang were sitting around a table eating pasties. Angie, Didier, Wim,

Christian and Stefan. Patrick said something about The Magnificent Fucking Seven. David settled everyone down, saying they were more like The Temperance Seven. He asked Stefan to gag Angie. ‘OK, I need everyone's help. This meeting is the final stage. The municipal elections are on Sunday, and between now and Sunday, I want you to convince or blackmail everybody you see to elect Trevor to the council. His election is vital. It should not be difficult as most of the residents of Plouyé like him anyway since he won his médaille d'honneur, so it's just a matter of combining our efforts. He’s an arrogant self-righteous dick-head, so once he’s in office, I’m sure he’ll stay. Well. He doesn't know yet, but legally, he must stay six years anyway. Oh, and by the way, where did those pasties come from?’

Angie, who had kept her mouth shut for a minute or two, piped up. ‘You have already involved me in a couple of your scams. How can I help? I live in Huelgoat, and anyway, Trevor cannot take office. He has to be a resident for five years.’

‘Don't worry about that Ang. The government have approved it. And most Plouyé residents go to your bar for one reason or the other!’

‘OK David, but only if you take me to Paris to see the movie.’

David smiled. ‘You're on.’

Angie was confused. ‘I'm not. I’ve got a fortnight to go.’

Now David was confused. He ignored her. He was still wondering if they were his pasties.

They all had a drink, and David wanted to thank everyone with a day out before voting day. Didier suggested Patrick's island. David had never heard of Patrick's island.

Patrick clarified. 'It's not called Patrick's fucking island. It's called I'le Stagadon. I named it after Don, the misses, who I met at a stag do. It's just a place to chill.' They all agreed to take a trip to the island on Saturday.

***

Saturday morning was here, and the day out to the seaside was to begin here and now. Trevor still didn't believe Patrick had an exclusive island. 'If he can afford an island, he can afford a new pair of jeans.'

'It's only a small island Trev. I think Didier said Patrick bought it when he bought Le Poher House. He made a ton of money in Australia as a sportsman. I think Didier send fencing. I'm not sure, cos I can't understand him. He's French you know.'

'Fencing? He misunderstood Patrick, you dick. He was a fence, a go-between, buying and selling stolen goods. Idiota'

'I think you mean idiot, Trev.'

'It's Latin, you Dodo, you're about as sharp as a sponge ball.'

The minibus arrived, full of idiots. Patrick was driving (everyone mad). Angie couldn't make it. She opened early on Saturdays. After the customary shaking of hands, they headed off to I'le Stagadon, and Patrick had a surprise. They were going to stop at a town on the way that David and Patrick would like. After going through Sizun, they came to a small seaside village and parked the bus. It was half-past ten and people were swimming in the freezing sea. Trevor thought this was funny. 'Anyone who goes swimming this time of the year must be in Seine.'

‘Now you Welsh fuckers, listen to this. Jean-Claude Le Tyrant is the name of the local Maire, and that's the fucking truth. Now have a look at that fucking sign.’

Trevor and David walked over to the village sign, and it read, DAOULAS.

‘Amazing, I don't believe it Trev. Is there a connection?’

‘No, the fucking place floods at high tide. There is a famous market here on Sunday's. The abbey is worth a visit. It has this fucking old garden with medicinal plants. You can get stoned for free. What the fuck, we better get on.’

Everyone hopped back on the bus heading for Plouguerneau where they joined the D71 for I'le Stagadon. David had a rare sensible thought. ‘If I'le Stagadon is an island, how do we board it?’

‘Board it! It's not a fucking ship, you Welsh twat. We get a fucking boat. My mate Claude will get us across. Board it! What a fucking pleb.’

Trevor quipped, ‘David could take a fence to that.’

David said, ‘I'm only trying to help.’

‘Yea, your fucking trying all right.’

Trevor told them to shut up before they have an accident. They reached a beach where Claude was waiting to ferry them across. Everyone shook hands. He could only take four at a time, so Trevor and Stefan waited. Trevor was worried as he couldn't swim unless he'd eaten mushrooms. Claude returned and took them across. The boat journey took about fifteen minutes. They reached the small island. Claude would come back at five o'clock to pick everyone up. Trevor was wondering why they didn't put the still here? It would have saved a fortune on bribes.

The longère (long-house) was situated close to the beach and surrounded by dunes and long grass. There were rabbits ducking and diving everywhere. Didier said, ‘they will haves le lapin pie pour le déjeuner, Mon Cheri.’

A longère is a traditional stone-built home, where humans and livestock (cattle or sheep) lived under a single roof. They can also be found on Bodmin Moor in Cornwall and in Wales where they’re called Ty Hir meaning long-house.

This longère was a long, single-storey gable-ended granite structure built lengthwise and slightly sloping. It divided into two rooms. Initially, humans occupied the higher end of the building, while the animals lived in the lower end. This was because cows and sheep cannot use toilets, so the slurry drains away. In Wales, the upper end was pen uchaf and the lower end pen isaf. Patrick used the top end as his living quarters and the lower end as his bedroom and bathroom. A wall and door separated them.

The house had no chimney. The smoke from the central fire filtered through the thatched roof and the whole space was open to the rafters, like a medieval English hall. Windows were tiny, so the interior was dark. David and Trevor were intrigued. There was a bumpy pitted floor on which stood three old wobbly settees and a large oblong table. There was a kitchen area with a sink and cupboard, but Patrick cooked over the open fire.

Didier brought his gun and had gone to get dinner. Patrick was lighting the tinder. He had a log store outside. They heard several loud bangs. Stefan said Didier was as blind as a bat so there would be no dinner. Patrick kept plenty of tinned food in the cupboard so that they wouldn't starve. Patrick had large tins of Irish Stew which would go into a big pot and put on the fire. Everyone was surprised when Didier returned with two rabbits. Patrick looked a bit surprised. 'I bet those little fuckers had already snuffed it.'

After rabbit stew, the drinking began. Patrick had the place stocked up and prepared for party time. They all got drunk and had a wonderful time as usual. Five o'clock arrived and Claude had to ferry a bunch of drunks across the river. Trevor insisted that he and David would wait for Captain Birdseye to return for them. This was because there were two cold lagers left.

***

It was Sunday morning. The last few days had been fruitful. The bar was all ready for the official opening on Saturday. It was local election day, and the Library was the polling station. It was the only time that many residents saw inside it. The polls were open until eight o'clock, but because of the small population, there was not much activity. David and Trevor were taking it easy. Angie kept repeating, 'Who's a pretty fucker then?' It got on David's nerves and gave him a headache.

Trevor was sitting on the pavement, as he was accustomed to doing when he saw something odd. Patrick's car pulled up outside the library. He and Didier were frog-marching people in. Patrick was shouting, 'Get the fuck in there and vote for your local hero.' They both jumped into the car and drove off. After a while, the whole episode repeated itself. The gendarme standing at the door to the library ignored all this commotion. Trevor never thought Patrick was so patriotic about France. He thought he must be daydreaming.

This procedure lasted all day. The library shuts just after eight PM. There were still people in the building late into the evening, who would be counting the votes for delivery to the Mairies the following morning. David lit the fire and settled down with a bottle of lager.

‘Who's a pretty fucker then?’

Trevor was polishing his shoes. He will have to attend the council meeting tomorrow, just to acknowledge the election of the new council. It should only be a quick meeting, then he could join David, and they could finish the electrics. It was no wonder places in France burned down. There was no earth, and electric cables hung around everywhere.

‘Dave, John the sparky wants to know if you prefer a rewire of the meter, neodymium rare earth magnets, or a borehole and pin.’

‘I like magnets Trev, once you remove them, everything looks normal to EDF. Just in case they come sniffing around when we’re busy.’

David bought some electrical goods from Patrick, some of which worked. They were English, so all the plugs were wrong. The microwave worked, and Patrick guaranteed it for another five years. Perran had given them a box of frozen pasties which they had been living on for the past few days. As the chest freezer was too big to go behind the bar, David had put a tablecloth over it and used it as a table. He thought it was common sense to combine the freezer with a table. There was a slight problem. When there were beers on it, every half an hour, it came on and vibrated, and this caused the beer to froth up. The French had never seen a vibrating table before! ‘Who's a pretty fucker then?’ ‘Shut up.’

***

# Breakfast at Taffies

Polly Golightly is a pretty, pretty girl
A parrot of distinction, a socialite pearl
Who often goes to Taffies for her breakfast or lunch
She will fly over tables for nibbles to munch

Polly Golightly was African born
So, when eating breakfast, she prefers corn
With just a few nuts, and maybe some fruit
When dining at Taffies, she looks so cute

Maire Trefor Dylan Jones

2018

# Chapter 19

Maire, Maire, Au Contraire.

Trevor was up early and walked around the corner to the Mairie building. He entered a room with a large table. There were several people seated, and others were arriving. Stefan, Jules, and Didier were sitting at the far end. Everyone stood and clapped him. One of them shouted, ‘Did you bring the médaille d'honneur pour acte de courage et de dévouement?’

‘No, of course not.’ Trevor felt a bit stupid, and he wished they didn't have to refer to it by its full name all the time. What was wrong with *medal.* There was handshaking everywhere. He asked Didier, ‘Why are we here.’ He thought Didier told him they were there to witness the election of the new councillors. Trevor thought these elections took place at the end of the month.

One wall had a huge three colour poster that resembled the French flag but with a women's face in the middle of it and the words Liberte, Egalite, and Fraternite, and below that in big letters REPUBLIQUE FRANCAISE. On another wall was a huge picture of President Hollande. Another wall had a big poster with some local information printed on it. He should have read it.

**Ville de Plouyé dans le département**
**Finistère (29)**
**Résultats des élections législatives 2014 dans la commune de Plouyé.**
**Consultez le résultat du 1er et 2ème tour avec la liste des candidats au poste de député pour la commune de Plouyé.**
**Résultats des élections Présidentielles 2014 dans la commune de Plouyé**
**Plouyé (29690) se trouve dans le département Finistère situé en région Bretagne.**
**(Dans le canton N°16 de Huelgoat. et la 6ème circonscription)**
**Le député de cette 6ème circonscription législative est Trefor Dylan Jones élu au 2ème tour avec un score de 58,36% avec la nuance politique Socialiste (SOC). (date de naissance :**
**01/04/1987, profession : Autre cadre (secteur privé))**
**La superficie de Plouyé est de 3755 hectares (37.55 km2) avec une altitude minimum de 67 mètres et un maximum de 246 mètres.**
**Plouyé est composée de 742 habitants (recensement publié en 2012) avec une densite de 19,76 personnes par km2.**
**Les citoyens de Plouyé sont nommés les Plouyéziens et les Plouyéziennes.**
**Plouyé (29690) est rattachée à la Communauté de communes du Yeun Ellez (numéro fiscal: 242900637).**

Everybody stood as the stocky little Maire walked in. He shook hands with Trevor and asked, 'Did you bring the médaille d'honneur pour acte de courage et de dévouement with you?'

'No.'

The Maire sat at the end of the table and nodded to Trevor. Trevor had found a seat next to Didier. He should be safe there. There was talking all around the table. Official papers were handed out and signed and dated. Didier showed Trevor where to sign and date. Trevor was confused. The Mayor adjourned the meeting for lunch. They were to resume at 10 am Wednesday morning. Trevor asked if he need attend. 'Oui, oui, of course,' Responded Didier.

'The thing is Didier, the Coreff barrels are arriving Wednesday morning, and I promised David I would help him with them.'

'That is OK, Patrick apportera les barils en. We will be long no, I mean we will not long be.' Everybody rushed off. Trevor and Didier got back to Penydarren.

***

It was Wednesday, and after a couple of quick lagers to help with the expectant boredom, Trevor returned to the Mairies for the resumption of the meeting. He couldn't understand a word or why he had to attend. After several people asked him if he had brought the médaille d'honneur pour acte de courage with him, they got down to business, and votes took place, and more papers were handed out for signatures. For some reason, Trevor had to sign, date, and give his French address and date of birth. He had to give this address as Penydarren was unsuitable. He gave his date of birth as the thirty-first of March 1987. Anything to get out of here. Didier asked Trevor. ‘It good you Maire now, Oui? It good for you.’ Trevor ignored him. Two young women entered the room with Champagne bottles and filled glasses with Champagne, and everyone toasted Trevor.

Claude the Maire, who was sitting at the top of the table delivered a short speech. He then turned to Trevor and spoke in English. ‘Trevor, we are all delighted that you have accepted the post as Mayor of Plouyé. It was a wise choice, and I salute you as your humble servant.’ Trevor was most confused and a little tipsy. Copies of a declaration, written in English for Claude's amusement, were handed to the members of the council.

‘Here Trevor is your copy of the declaration. I, Claude, will read the questions, and you Trevor will reply. It is all as clear as mud. You are now a Plouyezien, highly regarded in Brittany.’ Everybody drunk more Champagne.

Trevor had a think. 'What the hell. In for a Kopek, in for a Ruble'.

Members of the council elected the deputy Mayor at its first meeting. If there was not an out and out winner, the outcome could take several rounds of voting to conclude. Trevor was unaware that he had already been Le député Maire since Monday morning. All councillors had agreed to elected Trevor as the new Mayor of Plouyé. The Mayor had a six-year term, but nobody had told Trevor yet!

Claude. ‘Do you Trefor Dylan Jones solemnly promise and swear to govern the Peoples of the village of Plouyé and any of the belongings or pertaining, according to our respective laws and customs?'

Trevor. 'I solemnly promise so to do.'

Claude. 'And will you preserve unto the council of Plouyé, and to the Church there committed to their charge, all such rights and privileges, as by law do or shall appertain to them or any of them?'

Trevor. 'All this I promise to do. The things which I have here before promised, I will perform and keep. So help me God.'

Claude. 'You are now Maire of Plouyé. You will work from this building. There is a nice apartment upstairs, and if, after a few months you want to return to Wales, it will be OK. There is just one thing to remember. If you see me on the Street, I do not speak English.' Trevor might have been a bit tipsy, but he was sure he didn't mishear that! Maire? He didn't even know what he was supposed to do all day. Yes, he did consider putting his name forward as a Welsh councillor, but this was France, and he couldn't speak French.

He tried to explain to Claude. 'I'm Welsh. I cannot speak French. I know nothing of your system. I don't have a clue.'

'Do not worry. We have resolved that problem. Didier is your deputy Maire. He can be your translator.' Didier joined them.

Trevor was fuming, 'Didier, that idiot. He can't speak English, and he's stupid. No offence Didier.'

Didier grinned, 'Non defence takes.'

Trevor asked, 'Why can't Didier be Marie?'

Claude didn't have to think for long, 'He is stupid, sans vouloir offenser, Didier.'

Didier grinned again, 'Il n'y a pas de mal.

***

Saturday the fifteen of March. Last minute preparations. Trevor sent Didier to the pig farmer to pick up the bacon. Patrick would be bringing over a replacement microwave oven since the other one blew up that morning. The sound system was all working, and lots of the locals had donated CDs. All the stock was in place, and they even managed a deal with Coreff to supply barrels of Coreff Pression Brune et Ambree. Angie was going to help out behind the bar until David's French improved.

They opened at midday and were expecting a good crowd. David was in The Sports Bar buying a few boxes of cigarettes. Bar owners recommended not having ashtrays on display as to do so was considered brazen. If a bar had the luxury of a well-tiled floor, then you would often see vases or dish-like ornaments on the tables. David lit the fire. Trevor had a thought. 'David, my little unknowledgeable friend, did you know the Kipferl, ancestor of the croissant, was invented in Austria?' A high-pitched voice screamed from the corner of the room.

'Who's a pretty fucker then?' There was a shout in unison,

'Shut up.'

It was eleven thirty and people were arriving. David opened the door. It was too cold to leave them outside. So far Angie, David, Trevor, Claude(Maire), Wim, and seven others were drinking. Didier was in the factory making the first big batch of moonshine. Trevor was describing the declaration that took place yesterday. He joked:

'Will you to the utmost of your power maintain the small industry that supplies the peoples of Plouyé with the psychoactive effects of cannabis ruderalis, known to have a biphasic nature that will ensure relaxation among your peoples? Will you to the utmost of your power, maintain in Plouyé, the euphoria derived from tetrahydrocannabinol and Methanol? All this I promise to do. The things which I have here before promised, I will perform and keep. So help me God.'

***

More souls arrived, and by mid-afternoon, the place was rocking. Patrick was there with the new microwave, one that works. 'Who's a pretty fucker then?'

Patrick answered. He didn't often speak to parrots. 'You are, beaky, you little grey fucker.' Angie (New York) was talking so much that most of the customers went the long way around to get to the bar. Patrick spent a bit of time listening to her. 'Did you know Ang,' he said, 'behind every fat woman there is a slim one trying to get out. No seriously, you're in the way.'

People were playing daffodils (Bombardes), drums (bodhráns), and accordions. There were even double bass and a saxophone player. They took up most of the bar. Customers had spilt out into the road. All the council turned up. A couple of gendarmes came in laughing. They're Lieutenant de Police, who spent his spare time letting out vans and lorries had the radiator stolen from his biggest and newest lorry. When he finds the culprit, he is going to hang him from his balls and lock him up forever. Patrick looked nervous. Some of the French were playing a card game called Belote, but the table vibrated, and the cards fell on the floor. David distributed bacon sandwiches, and even the French were eating them. Trevor said he was on a pole-tree diet and shouldn't eat bacon sandwiches, but he could cheat occasionally, so he played cards with the French.

***

Trevor was outside talking to David about his new flat when he got the shock of his life. Who came over to say ça va (How are you)? None other than Madame Martine Rousseau. She looked at Trevor. 'I'll come clean. I'm here to thank you beautiful men, for stealing my precious stones. Oh yes, I know it was you. I know quite a few people in Huelgoat, and I was assured that if it was anyone, it was you two.' David blushed. She went on. 'Don't worry, your secret is safe with me, you see you have done me a favour. You must know by now that they were fake. Well, my insurance company didn't, and paid me in full, so it was the best thing that could have happened. I had better get you both a drink.' She walked into the bar. David and Trevor were astonished. 'Trev, how does she know we won't go to the police?'

'David, my little Venus flytrap, how can we go to the police? *We* stole them.'

She returned with two glasses of champagne for them.

David was surprised, he asked, 'Who got the Champagne?'

Martine smiled, 'I have a friend, Aissa, who works in the café at Roscoff port. He visits his mother in Chalon, Champagne every month and gets me cheap Champagne and wine. I brought you a couple of boxes for your trouble, cheers boys.' She wandered back into the bar.

They sat on the pavement, flabbergasted. David thought it was time he also came clean.

'Don't get mad Trev, but when I arrived, the first person I met was Claude, the Maire. We became close friends. He is half English on his mother's side and speaks it fluently although he fervently denies this. He offered me this place for a song as it was a ruin. The village needed a bar, as Wim's is a shop. Now that Plouyé has such a high percentage of foreign residents the Maire must be English speaking. Due to this, and Claude's impending retirement, he has been advised by the Ministre de l'Intérieur, Manuel Valls, that if no one in residency is suitable for the job, he can offer it to an outsider who has given exceptional service to France. No pre-existing residency requirement is necessary. When you won the medal for bravery, it was the icing on the cake. You had performed an act of exceptional service to France. Apart from the local benefits of having an English-speaking Maire, it is also in the Nations interest to employ more English people in local government. When we were discussing local affairs, I happened to mention you and your passion for local government and your interest in local councils. We agreed that if I supplied the Maire, the council would give me a thousand euros to convert this old house into a thriving new bar. We had to keep you here long enough for you to get to like it, and to meet new friends. Sorry Trev, but I didn't want you to go home. Let's share the bar and the Maires work.'

Trevor was gobsmacked. 'You little Welsh bastard. What about the fire in the bar?'

'What fire? I could never afford an up and running bar. It was just a burned-out house, and I could afford that. I wasted a lot of my donkey winnings on food and beer. Patrick said that you would never notice that there were no bar signs outside, although he nearly gave the game away when you two first met. He asked if you were here to help me with my old burnt out house, and when you first saw the building, you said something like*, I was expecting loads of ash and the smell of burnt wood.* I said it had been very windy.' David laughed.

'David, my little Welsh Prince of darkness, I have the authority to shut this place down, and I might just do that, and get you all locked up for distilling illegal spirits.'

'Oh, a bit of a problem there Trev. There are fifteen reliable witnesses and two CCTV cameras that can verify you as the jewel thief. You will be defrocked of your medal, and they will lock you up with the DJ's and bum hunters.'

'David, I can always spot a leopard by its stripes. Oh, what the hell. We might as well give it a go.'

'Good old Trev. It was all supposed to be a lot simpler than it was. I wasn't to know you were going to keep getting banged up like a Welsh prostitute. I might even write a book about the whole experience.'

Trevor believed it must be destiny. 'If you do, you must get my poems into print as well.'

'OK Trev, perhaps we can *combine* the two into one book.

Trevor slapped his head, as he often did, 'I could add a poem to the end of each chapter. I will call myself by my birth name, Trefor Dylan Jones. And what about you Dave my little singing kettle, you will need a psycho name?'

David had a thought. 'I always liked Barry. Mum said I was conceived under the pier at Barry Island.'

Trevor smiled, 'You are blessed, my son, and what about a surname Dave? What's your favourite song?'

'That's obvious Trev, *Going Home*.' Trevor did not like the name Barry Going Home. David had a little think, 'My second favourite is *Child in Time* by Deep Purple. Barry Child sounds OK.'

Trevor wasn't convinced. 'It sounds childish.'

'OK Trev, Barry Childs. That's my final offer.'

The following morning was clean-up time for David. Trevor was in the library searching for anything related to the Ville de Plouyé dans le département Finistère (29). It was going to be fun listening to Didier's translation. Trevor had already received an application for the erection of a wind turbine on a local farm. It was early days so he will have to ask Claude for advice on how many bottles of wine the farmer would have to cough-up.

In the afternoon the entrepreneurs relaxed. David phoned his parents and told them the good news. All four of them will be flying over to visit next week. David will meet them at Brest Airport. David's mother told him how proud they all were.

'Dave, did you know the only other British Mayor in France is a Yorkshire-man? Ken Tatham, who has been the mayor of Saint Céneri-le-Gérei for a very long time.

There was singing in the bar. It was Patrick and the parrot. 'Who's a pretty fucker then?' As they walked back into the bar, they heard what sounded like an explosion coming from the distance in the general direction of Penker Lois. Trevor slapped his head.

The End

‘What do you mean, the end?’

‘The book is finished Trev, so it’s the end.’

‘David, my little cheating hyena, you promised me that I would have a poem after each chapter.’

‘And so you have.’

‘Well, I don’t see any poem here, unless it is hiding in the footer somewhere.’

Trev, it is *The End*! How can you have a poem after the end?’

‘You better start calling me Monsieur Maire, David. Anyway, I could put my poem in and then you could write*, The End.’*

‘The end goes at the end of the novel, not the end of the poetry, if that’s what you call it. Anyway, your so-called poetry is crap Trevor. Oh, and by the way, if I have to call you Maire, you can call me Barry.’

‘Barry is not your real name, twat, it is only your psycho name, while Monsieur Maire is my official title.’

‘OK, Mr know-all Maire, if your poems are so good, how come we have only sold three copies of the book so far? Your one, my one, and my mum’s one. Even your parents didn’t want one.’

‘Well, Mr airy fairy Barry David bollock chops, if we have only sold three copies, it would suggest to me that your novel writing skills are right down there with my poem writing skills. I’m going to bed.’

‘Goodnight Trev boy.’ ‘Goodnight Dave boy.’

‘

26056804R00129

Printed in Poland
by Amazon Fulfillment
Poland Sp. z o.o., Wrocław